THE FORGOTTEN TALE

THE ROAD TO HELL

A Territorial War Story
By: Lewis D McDonald

PREQUEL

<u>**Thank you**</u> for giving this tale of mine a read. This is a prequel to a spinoff series that is based on a TTRPG campaign that my friends and I are running in the same setting as the "Territorial War" story. I have thoroughly enjoyed building up Paxanthus with a level of depth it never had before, as well as exploring a time that goes mostly unmentioned in Paxanthus' history.

If you enjoy this story and are interested in reading more, please give any of the other books I have written a try! I love to hear feedback, whether good or bad, so shoot me a message on any of the socials if you'd like.

The Territorial War Series:
Territorial War - The Legends of Old (prequel)
Territorial War - The Birth of Evil (prequel)
Territorial War - (Book 1)
Territorial War - A Battle on Two Fronts (Book 2)
Territorial War - The End of an Era (Book 3)
Territorial War - A Fight for Survival (Book 4)

The Lands of War Collection:
The Plague of Kavronax
The Rise of a King
The Death of the Shroud
The Battle of Fates

The Forgotten Tale Series:
The Forgotten Tale - The Road to Hell (prequel)
The Forgotten Tale - The Island of Cirantha (Book 1)
The Forgotten Tale - For the Good of the People (Book 2)
The Forgotten Tale - Beneath a Perilous Veil (Book 3)
The Forgotten Tale - A Tragedy in Pasea (Book 4)
The Forgotten Tale - Dancing with the Devil (Book 5)
The Forgotten Tale - The Truth Unfolds (Book 6)
The Forgotten Tale - The Death of a Fiend (Book 7)

Follow the series on Social Media at:

Instagram - **@territorial_war**
Facebook - **https://www.facebook.com/TerritorialWar**
TikTok - **@territorial_war**

If you enjoy the story, please leave a review and spread the word!

Pronunciation Guide

Some of the words in this book might be a little out of the ordinary. Refer back to this guide if you need to see how any of the words are pronounced when you see them!

Locations
Altomir = ALL-toe-meer

People
Aria = ARE-re-uh
Bokon = BO-con
Dargothur = DARR-guh-thurr
Ehrindil = AIR-in-dill
Evonna = e-VAHN-uh
Junius = JOO-nee-us

Preface

Large-scale battles have a lot of moving parts and it can be difficult to organize and describe the actions of an individual in a moment of time when many individuals are involved. To help provide more clarity, in this book you are going to see breaks in the fight like this:

~   ~   ~   ~   ~   ~   ~   ~

This break indicates the perspective shifting from one area of the battle to another. This makes it easier to describe what each individual(s) may be doing at a moment in time without creating a confusing paragraph that jumps between too many people and dilutes the perspective.

Multiple moments will be happening within the same period, and breaking the battles up in this fashion will help describe these moments with more clarity. I hope this helps!

Chapter 1

The air was cool and calm, and the sounds of rushing water filled the ears of anyone outside. There was a river with southern-moving waters that ran alongside the western side of a small farmstead. The river flowed crystal-clear waters that trickled down from the mountain range to the north, providing the people downstream with fresh water to drink.

A cloud cover obscured the sun, but the area was still well-lit, with plenty of daylight to get some work done around the farm. A young man named Junius Wildheart tended the fields on his farmstead named Alcombey. He was a hard-working man who wanted nothing more than to provide for his family. His wife and daughter lived with him, and they cared for the home while he toiled in the fields.

He was gathering the last bit of corn from a recent harvest when he spotted a small pillar of smoke in the distance to the northwest. His worry grew as he watched the smoke stretch high into the clouds, as he knew a large fire had to be the source. He remembered that a small town called Woodpine had been established there, but he only visited it once or twice. He hoped everyone was alright.

"Junius!" a woman yelled out. "Dinner will be done soon, dear."

"I'm coming, hun!" Junius yelled back to his wife.

He looked back at the pillar of smoke one more time before turning for his home for a nice warm meal to end the day. As he walked through the door, he was immediately greeted with the delicious smell of fresh stew and the smiling faces of his wife and daughter.

"That smells amazing, Evonna," Junius said.

"It's rabbit and carrot stew, I know it's your favorite," Evonna replied. "Have a seat, I'll get us all a bowl."

"Daddy!" a young girl said excitedly as she sat at the table.

"Yes, Aria?" Junius responded.

"I made something for you," Aria said as she grabbed a piece of paper and held it out for Junius to take.

Junius grabbed the paper and looked it over. It was a crudely drawn picture of a young kid and two adults standing in front of a house in the background.

"It's us!" Aria said. "So that way you can remember us when you go to town on your long trips."

"Aria, this is impressive for someone your age. Who would have guessed we had a four-year-old artist in the house? But I could never forget you, even without the picture. You're all I think about from the moment I leave," Junius said with a warm smile as he hugged Aria. "Now grab a seat, it's time to eat."

"Grab a seat, it's time to eat. Grab a seat, it's time to eat," Aria sang as she danced her way back to her seat.

Junius smiled as he looked around at his home. It wasn't much, but it had everything they needed to survive. And most importantly, it had everything he cared about living within. He looked back down at the paper for a moment before folding it up and placing it inside his chest pocket.

"Here you go, dear," Evonna said as she set a bowl down in front of him.

"Oh, I can barely contain my excitement," Junius said jokingly as he grabbed a spoon and waited for Evonna.

Once his wife sat down and started to eat, he did the same. He took a bite of the food, and his taste buds were sent on a rollercoaster. The broth was flavorful, and the rabbit was succulent. It was truly his favorite thing to eat.

"Thank you, dear," Junius said as he took a second bite.

"Of course," Evonna responded. "You're going to need your energy. You have a big trip ahead of you tomorrow."

"Yeah," Junius agreed as his expression slowly shifted.

Evonna let out a sigh and asked, "You're worried about something. What is it?"

"It's the bandits. They're getting closer and closer by the day. I've seen stragglers in town already, so I know they're coming in force soon enough. When they get here, I don't know what they'll take," Junius said with worry.

"It will be okay," Evonna assured. "They haven't expanded their territory across the river for as long as I've been alive."

"That doesn't mean they won't," Junius debated.

"Well, if that day comes, then we'll figure out a plan then," Evonna stated.

"I worry they've already made it to Woodpine," Junius said. "I saw a pillar of smoke coming from that direction. I know the Clan of Phantoms has been threatening a hostile takeover of Woodpine for years now. I wonder if it finally happened."

"Let's hope for their sake it hasn't. The other factions have been giving the Clan of Phantoms a lot to deal with. If they can keep all the violence amongst one another, the rest of us can live safely," Evonna said hopefully.

"I hope you're right, dear. I would hate to have anything disrupt what we have," Junius said with a smile. "But, if they do come, we should leave. I know you hate when I talk about it, but we should have a solid plan in place so we aren't scrambling to decide in an emergency."

"Where would we go?" Evonna asked.

"I don't know. But Bradley told me that he found a portal in the woods to the east. We could leave Altomir altogether and maybe find a world where criminals aren't in charge," Junius offered.

"How do we know a world like that even exists?" Evonna asked. "It seems so risky. What if where it takes us is worse?"

Junius let out a defeated sigh before saying, "You're probably right. Power is corrupting, so everywhere is probably similar to here. I just know that fleeing to the east will only lead us to different criminals. I don't know, I guess I just wish there were a way to escape all of this."

Evonna leaned over and wrapped her arms around Junius as she rested her head on his shoulders, saying, "I know, dear. But don't worry, we will all be okay. We will tackle any obstacle we face together, and we will get through it."

Junius felt his heart warm as he rested his head in hers and said, "Thank you. I couldn't do this without you."

"Daddy," Aria said suddenly after she finished eating, "Can you tell me a bedtime story tonight?"

"Of course," Junius agreed. "But only one."

"Yay!" Aria said as she clapped her hands.

"But first, we must clean up our mess," Evonna instructed.

"We clean our bowls and wash our hands," Aria agreed.

"That's right," Evonna said with a smile.

"She's smarter than both of us, you know that, right?" Junius mumbled.

"As long as she doesn't know that, we'll be fine," Evonna whispered back.

The two shared a laugh before finishing their meals and cleaning up their dishes. After they finished, they could see the sun had already vanished behind the horizon. Junius picked up Aria and carried her to her bed to tuck her in.

"What's the story about?" Aria asked excitedly.

"Let's see," Junius responded. "How about a story about a princess?"

"I love princess stories!" Aria exclaimed. "Because I'm going to be a princess one day."

"I'm sure you will," Junius chuckled. "Now settle in. There once was a princess who had everything she could have ever wanted. She was beautiful, wealthy, and people loved her. However, she was sometimes mean to people and would call them names, especially people who didn't look like her.
One day, she saw a man with a disfigured face, and she laughed and pointed at him, calling him ugly. What she didn't know was that she was insulting a troll in disguise. The troll kidnapped the princess and took her from her kingdom. He locked her away at the top of a tower and put a curse on her."

"A curse?" Aria said, scared.

"Yes, a curse that turned her into a devilkin when the sun went down," Junius answered.

"With scary horns?" Aria asked.

"Yes, long horns, red skin, and fiery eyes," Junius replied. "She hated devilkin because she thought they were evil demons."

"But they're not," Aria said, shaking her finger.

"That's right, but she didn't think that. At night, she would look at herself in the mirror and despise the troll for what he did, but there was nothing she could do. Until one day, she heard the sounds of fighting from the bottom of the tower. She was scared and didn't know what was going on, but eventually a man in shiny knight armor walked through the door and said he was there to rescue her.

She thanked him over and over as they went back down the tower and out the door. However, the trip back home would take several days, and she didn't want the brave knight to see her devilkin form, so she told him to stay away from her after the sun went down.

During the day, they laughed, talked, and discovered they had a lot in common. He taught her to catch food, and she taught him to cook. They were falling in love, but the knight had kept his armor on the entire time. The only things she could see were his eyes behind a small slit in his visor.

She asked him to take off his helmet because she wanted to see the man with whom she had so much in common, but he didn't want to. He said he was worried she wouldn't like the way he looks, but she insisted. So, he took off his helmet and revealed himself to be a devilkin," Junius said with suspense.

Aria gasped and asked, "And then what happened?"

"You'll have to wait until next time to hear the end," Junius said with a wink. "It's late, and we need to sleep too."

"Awww," Aria said with a pouty face. "Okay…"

"I love you, Aria," Junius said as he kissed her on the forehead. "Goodnight, and sleep sweet."

"Goodnight, Aria," Evonna said as she did the same.

"Goodnight, mommy and daddy," Aria replied as she snuggled into her blanket.

Junius and Evonna smiled as they walked over to their bed and got comfortable under the blanket. They snuggled up to one another and felt the warmth of each other's bodies as they relaxed.

"How long do you think you'll be gone?" Evonna asked.

"Hopefully, less than a week. Coniston is only two days away, and I don't plan to stay in town longer than it takes me to sell," Junius answered.

"Hurry back, we miss you when you're not here," Evonna pleaded.

"Don't worry, I promise to come back as fast as I can; everything I could ever want is here anyway," Junius said with a smile.

Evonna rested her head on his chest and listened to his heartbeat as her head rose and fell with each breath he took. He had his arm wrapped around her shoulders and held her close; her soft skin was a comforting contrast to the rough tools his hands usually held. He traced his fingers along her back as they lay there, and she could hear his heartbeat slowly getting faster.

She looked up at him with a devilish smirk, as she knew what he was thinking. She leaned in closer to kiss him. As she did, she slid her leg across his body and pulled herself on top of him. He welcomed her passionately as they embraced one another beneath the covers. They enjoyed every moment they could squeeze out of the twilight hours before they had to sleep, as the morning came early and waited for no one.

The following day, Junius rose with the sun and was packing his wagon with crops to take to town and trade. He had taken this trip hundreds of times over the years, so he was familiar with the route and expected a smooth journey. He had the wagon packed full and ready to go, so he walked back inside to say his goodbyes.

"Okay, I'm headed off now," Junius said as he knelt next to Aria. "Be good for mommy, okay?"

"I will," Aria answered.

"I know you will," Junius said with a grin before standing and walking toward Evonna.

"I meant what I said last night, hurry home," Evonna said as she poked him playfully on the chest.

"I'll go as fast as old Ippy will carry me," Junius promised.

"You should get a younger horse, maybe that will save you some time," Evonna offered.

"We don't have the money for a younger horse. Besides, Ippy has been making these trips with me for years. I could never do him like that," Junius denied.

"Just consider it," Evonna smiled. "But be careful, please."

"I always am," Junius assured. "I'll be home before you know it. Is there anything you need from town while I'm there?"

"Some fresh beef would be nice if you sell well. We haven't had anything other than rabbit and venison for a while," Evonna answered.

"I'll make sure to get it," Junius said with a nod. "I love you."

"I love you, too, Junius," Evonna said.

He wrapped his arms around her and kissed her before saying his goodbye and stepping back outside. He walked over to his wagon and climbed into his seat before looking back over his shoulder at his house. He didn't enjoy leaving, but he knew it had to be done. Without selling their excess crops, they wouldn't be able to afford the other things they needed. So, he grabbed the reins, mushed Ippy along, and the horse started to pull the wagon away from the farmstead.

Chapter 2

The trip to Coniston was lengthy but peaceful. Junius would pass the time by watching the wildlife or whistling a tune. At night, he would carve little figures out of pieces of wood to give to Aria, even if she always broke them. He even took some time to look at the picture she had drawn of them.

He had been on the road for a couple of days and knew he would be in Coniston within an hour or two. He was ready to get there and sell his goods so he could start his trip back, but he noticed something odd in the distance. Four men were standing in the roadway, and they didn't appear to be moving.

Junius began to worry, but there was no way around the men. The closer he traveled, the easier it was to see them, and he could tell they were armed with swords and bows. He slowed down his wagon once he saw the weapons, and was about to turn around when he heard a voice suddenly speak out from right next to him.

"Don't even think about runnin'. Just keep going," the man said threateningly.

The man who spoke climbed up on the side of the wagon and pressed a dagger against Junius' neck, motioning him to keep going toward the other men. Junius immediately was riddled with anxiety. He knew these men were bandits and could smell the blood on their clothes. However, aside from a hunting bow and a skinning knife, he was unarmed and unable to defend himself. Junius kept the wagon going until he got closer to the other bandits and was ordered to stop.

"That's enough, now let go of the reins," the man ordered.

Junius slowly placed the reins down and raised his arms to show he had no intention of trying to fight. He hoped his pacifist approach would be the least provoking way to get through whatever was about to happen.

One of the men who was standing in the road stepped forward and said, "Get down here and we won't kill you."

Junius nodded and slowly made his way down off the wagon. He looked at the man and asked, "What's going on?"

"We'll ask the questions here," the leader barked. "What do you have in the wagon? And don't even think about lyin'."

"I have corn, that's about it," Junius answered.

"That's all you have? Corn?" the leader growled.

"Yes, I swear," Junius assured.

"Go and look," the leader said to the others.

The other three men with him walked to the back of the wagon and ripped the cloth off the back, revealing a large stash of corn piled up and ready for sale. They grabbed a few pieces and opened them up to check the freshness, and found they were harvested at the perfect time.

"Nothin' but corn back here," one of the men shouted from the back. "Good stuff too."

"Oh yeah?" the leader yelled back. "He must be from that farm up the road. Take what you can carry."

Junius looked at the back of the wagon and then back at the man next to him, but didn't say anything. He was angry, but there was nothing he could do about it.

"Is that gonna be a problem?" the leader asked as he leaned in toward Junius.

"N-no," Junius answered as he lowered his head.

"You should be thankin' us, we're just lightenin' the load on your poor horse," the leader said with a laugh. There was a long and awkward pause before the man spoke again aggressively, "I said, you should be thankin' us."

Junius looked at him in confusion, but then pieced together what he wanted. He gritted his teeth and replied, "Thank you."

"For what?" the leader asked.

"For lightening the load on my horse," Junius said through clenched teeth.

"You hear that, boys? He's thankin' us for this," the man shouted to the rest of them, trying to humiliate Junius.

"What a coward," one of the others yelled back.

"We don't like cowards," the leader grunted before he slammed his fist into Junius' stomach.

Junius fell to the ground coughing and ashamed as the men all laughed at him. They grabbed as much corn from the back of his wagon as they could carry and left him on the dirt road behind them. He was fuming with anger and riddled with shame, but he was alive. He walked to the back of his wagon and grabbed the torn cloth to put it inside. He looked at his produce and saw that they had taken about a third of what he wanted to sell, but there was still enough to make the trip worthwhile, so he hopped back on his wagon and continued into town.

As he arrived in Coniston, his pride, as well as his abdomen, was bruised, but he was happy to see some familiar faces. Coniston wasn't a very large town, but it had anything anyone could want or need. He continued toward the market and stopped his wagon at his usual spot before he pulled out a stand and set some of his produce on top for display. His goods were known to be fresh and flavorful, so he immediately attracted people who wanted to start buying.

One of the people who approached was his friend Bradley. Bradley was a butcher, and they regularly traded crops for fresh meat. Junius was happy to see his friend, but he could tell something was wrong as Bradley approached.

"How are you, Junius?" Bradley said with a wave.

"I've had better days," Junius answered. "How about you?"

"I could say the same," Bradley answered. "You don't have as much as you usually do, selling out that fast? Make sure to save some for me."

"I wish, but no. I was robbed on my way in," Junius answered with his head hung.

"What? Are you okay?" Bradley asked with worry.

"Yes, they didn't do much to me or Ippy, they just took a good chunk of my crops," Junius answered.

"I'm sorry, Junius," Bradley said. "Things are getting harder around here for everyone. It would seem the Clan of Phantoms is making their way across the river now."

"What? Already?" Junius asked.

"Yes. Some stragglers are already here in Coniston. I've seen them staying nearby. Apparently, Bokon has nearly wiped out the other three factions," Bradley answered. "I heard he even killed Magnus Corvus."

"Bokon?" Junius said with confusion.

"Yes, the leader of the Clan of Phantoms. I thought you knew that," Bradley clarified.

"No, I only knew of Magnus and Burgrunde. They're the ones that are closest to my home," Junius responded.

"Well, apparently, Bokon has been telling his people to push farther east. I figured with Sanctuary being so far away, we wouldn't have to deal with this," Bradley expressed.

"I knew it would happen eventually, I just thought we had more time," Junius added. "What does he want with the land out here?"

"What anyone wants, power," Bradley answered. "The more towns he has, the more influence he has, the more supplies he has, and then some."

"It's not safe here anymore, Bradley. We should leave and put this place and the Clan of Phantoms behind us. The risk of staying is too great," Junius offered. "What about that portal you mentioned? Let's go through it."

"I can't, I am too old to be traveling the realms," Bradley dismissed. "But you, you are at the perfect age to start over. Take Evonna and Aria and get away from here before it's too late. It's only a matter of time before they get here in force, and just because you live farther away won't mean you're safe. The portal isn't far from where you live. I found it near the great willow tree, underneath a mangled root."

"Okay, I understand. I wish you would come with us, but I won't drag you by your ears," Junius said with a chuckle. "Make sure to have some beef ready, I'll come by there before sundown. I may need the quality food to convince Evonna to leave."

"I'll have the usual ready for you," Bradley said with a grin.

The next few hours passed by quickly, and Junius sold nearly every last bit of his food, except for what he set aside for Bradley. After the last bit of stock was purchased, he packed up his wagon and tied off Ippy to a post so he wouldn't leave.

He spent a little time traveling from shop to shop, gathering supplies they would need for their journey and stocking up on items they were low on. He even traded with a wandering merchant whom he had seen from time to time, but the man didn't have much more than various curiosities. His nerves were on edge, and he was scared of what awaited them on the other side of the portal, but he wanted to get his family as far away from the coming danger as possible. He estimated they had plenty of time to figure out a plan, but if they're already showing up at Coniston, it was only a matter of time before they came to take over. The tricky part would be convincing Evonna that they should go.

After he traded some gold for supplies, he made his way over to Bradley's butchery and dropped off the last bit of his corn. Bradley loaded a slab of beef onto the back of his wagon that was much larger than usual. Junius looked at him with confusion, but Bradley waved his hand in dismissal.

"Don't mention it. Consider it a parting gift," Bradley stated.

"Are you sure you don't want to come with us?" Junius asked. "We could use your skills on the road."

"I'm sure, Junius, but I appreciate your concern. I'm just an old man, even when they get here, I doubt they'll bother me much. It's easier to weather that than it is to pack up and leave the only home I've ever known," Bradley dismissed.

"I'll miss you, Bradley. It's been a pleasure over the years," Junius said as he placed his hand on Bradley's shoulder.

"Yeah, yeah, don't get mushy on me," Bradley teased. "I'll miss you, too, kid. Go and take care of your family. We'll be alright here, we knew this was coming eventually."

Junius gave a nod and hopped back onto his wagon. He hurried Ippy along, and the old horse started to pull the wagon as fast as he could. Junius was desperate to get back home and see his family. If it weren't for the horse needing his rest, he would have traveled all through the night.

On his way back out of town, he was worried that he might run back into the bandits who had robbed him before, but luckily, they were nowhere to be seen. He did spot some tracks heading away from the road and into the woods, so he assumed they were out of the way. Aside from the singular set of tracks, he saw nothing else the rest of the day.

Sleeping that night was difficult. He feared there would be trouble lurking in the darkness, but eventually he grew too tired to fight it. He awoke the next morning as the sun's rays warmed his cheeks, and gasped as he realized he overslept. He quickly looked around, but it was nothing but him and Ippy in the area.

He let out a sigh of relief and looked right at Ippy, saying, "Why didn't you wake me up?"

Ippy just looked at him and neighed. Junius shook his head, stood up, rolled up his sleeping mat, and packed up his things to get back on the road. If he traveled quickly, he figured he could make it back home by nightfall.

The day was long, but he kept going. He rewarded Ippy with some carrots a few times throughout the trip, as he knew the old stallion wasn't used to pulling all day. But as sure as the sun would rise in the morning, Junius made it home as the day was coming to an end.

He released Ippy into his pen and grabbed some things from the wagon before he walked inside. As he stepped through the door, Evonna jumped to her feet and grabbed Aria.

"I'm sorry, I didn't mean to scare you," Junius said.

"Daddy!" Aria exclaimed as she ran toward him.

"Hello, sweetheart," Junius said as he knelt to hug her.

"I wasn't expecting you until tomorrow at the earliest," Evonna said.

"I moved quickly today," Junius explained. "I was ready to see your beautiful faces."

Evonna looked at him for a second, then said, "I can tell something is wrong. What happened?"

"Your intuition is admirable," Junius said with a smirk. "I brought some beef. Why don't we have a good meal, and I'll tell you everything. I'll help cook."

"If you insist," Evonna said as she walked over and gave Junius a hug and kiss.

The two of them spent some time making dinner and enjoying each other's company. It didn't take long for them to have some steaks cooked, accompanied by steamed vegetables on the side. It was a meal fit for royalty. They sat down and started to eat their food, soaking in every delicious bite until none was left, when Aria pulled on Junius' sleeve.

"Daddy, will you tell me the rest of the story tonight?" Aria asked.

"Of course," Junius agreed. "I have left you waiting for nearly a week already."

"It is time for bed now. Why don't you carry her to her room? I'll clean up here." Evonna suggested.

Junius agreed and picked up Aria to carry her to bed. He sat her down and pulled the blanket up to her neck, then pressed the covers underneath her to tuck her in tight. He then grabbed a seat right next to the bed and cleared his throat.

"Alright, where was I?" Junius asked.

"You were telling me that the knight was really a devilkin," Aria answered.

"Right," Junius said, "So, the princess ran away and hid herself in a nearby cave. The brave knight followed her to make sure she was safe, because the sun was starting to set, and bears lived where they were. He ran after her and found the cave where she had hidden.

He could hear the sounds of a bear growling from deeper in the cave, so he ran in to protect the princess. He found her with her back against the wall, and a massive bear slowly bearing down on her."

"Oh no!" Aria gasped.

"He charged the bear with his sword drawn and cut the beast down to save the princess, but he was hurt in the fight. The battle was long, but eventually the brave knight emerged victorious.

He turned to see the princess, but was baffled to find another devilkin wearing her clothing. He demanded to know where the princess had gone, but she assured him it was her. It took some time to convince him, but eventually he could tell she was telling the truth. The devilkin in front of him was the princess.

She ran toward him and wrapped her arms around him to thank him for saving her. She explained that she was cursed and that she was startled when she saw him. She could never see herself loving a devilkin, but she fell in love with one. That was when her life changed. She kissed the knight and turned entirely into a devilkin. She spent the rest of her life with the brave knight, and they lived happily ever after," Junius finished.

"That is such a pretty story," Aria said with a smile. "I will be a devilkin princess one day."

"We'll see about that," Junius said with a laugh. "Get some sleep, Aria. I'll see you in the morning."

"Goodnight, daddy," Aria said as she snuggled in.

"Goodnight, Aria," Junius said as he kissed her on the forehead.

Junius walked away to rejoin Evonna and helped her finish cleaning up the remaining items from dinner. They were cleaning some of the dishes together when she gave him a look out of the corner of her eye.

"Are you going to tell me what happened now?" Evonna asked.

"I think we should leave," Junius said bluntly.

"What? We talked about this before you left," Evonna sighed.

"I know, but it's happening," Junius responded. "The Clan of Phantoms is already here. They have been lurking around Coniston already, Bradley told me."

"Are you sure you can believe him? Bradley isn't known to be the most rational," Evonna argued calmly.

"Yes, I saw them too. I was robbed on my way into town," Junius said with defeat in his voice.

"What? What happened, love? Are you okay?" Evonna asked with worry.

"I'm fine," Junius brushed off. "My pride was hurt more than anything."

"What did they take? Did they hurt you?" Evonna asked as she started to lift Junius' shirt.

"They only took some corn, and they didn't hurt me," Junius said.

Evonna lifted his shirt enough to see the bruise on his abdomen and then looked at him blankly, saying, "Junius, I'm so sorry."

"I'm fine. This is nothing compared to what they could have done, and I don't want to risk that happening," Junius expressed.

Evonna looked him in the eyes and could see the worry he carried. She could tell he meant what he said and understood the danger the Clan of Phantoms was to cross. She let out a reluctant sigh as she thought about what to say.

"Okay. I think you're right. But where would we go?" Evonna asked.

"I think we should try the portal. It is a gateway between realms; it could take us to a land far safer than here. Then we won't have to worry about ever dealing with these bandits again," Junius explained.

"It's so risky, Junius. What if we can't come back?" Evonna asked.

"I know it is, but I just have a feeling that whatever is on the other side is our ticket to peace. We just have to take the risk," Junius expressed

Evonna thought about it for a moment before saying, "Okay. I trust you. What should we pack?"

"Nothing more than we can carry. Maybe some food and camping supplies, just enough to get us through a week or so," Junius answered. "The portal is less than a day away, and I bought some items that may help us. Bradley said it's next to the great willow in the eastern forest."

"Okay, dear. I'll gather some things. We should let Aria rest for the night and leave in the morning," Evonna suggested.

"That sounds like a good plan. I'll help pack," Junius agreed.

They spent the next hour gathering food and packing a few essentials that they might need for the trip. They didn't think too hard about it, as they could only carry so much, and the wagon would never make it into the forest. After they packed what they needed, they settled into bed and did their best to rest their minds and bodies. However, it wasn't easy, because the following morning would be the last one in their home.

Chapter 3

The next morning, Junius and Evonna were putting the final touches on their bags for their trip when they saw Aria come into the room, rubbing her eyes. She looked at them with a confused look as she sauntered toward them.

"Mommy, Daddy, what's going on?" Aria asked.

"We're going to go on a trip," Junius said with a smile.

"When will we be coming back?" Aria questioned.

Junius and Evonna looked at one another for a brief moment before Evonna answered, "We won't be, sweetheart. We're going to go somewhere new and find a new home."

"Really? Why?" Aria continued.

"Because we think there is a better one out there for us," Junius said with a smile, trying to be as comforting as possible.

"So grab a few of your favorite toys to bring with us, okay?" Evonna instructed. "I'll get you some breakfast ready while you do."

"Okay, mommy," Aria replied as she went back toward her room.

"Are you ready to go?" Junius asked. "Is there anything else that needs to be packed or stored away?"

"No, I think that's it," Evonna answered. "What about Ippy?"

"He's worked enough," Junius said with a grin, "Like you said, he's earned his retirement. There is plenty of grass in his field for him to live off of until he passes. He will be just fine without us."

"Okay, I'll get Aria some food, and we will be ready to leave," Evonna said. "I hope this works out."

"I do, too, love. I really do," Junius replied.

Evonna threw together a quick meal for Aria and gave her a moment to eat before they gathered their belongings and left their home. They took one last look behind them before leaving to soak in the view. Everything they had worked for, built, and known was on this land, and it was difficult to walk away. However, they knew it was time.

They left the farmstead and started for the eastern forest, disappearing behind the treeline and walking deeper into the woods. The great willow was visible from quite far away, as it was the tallest tree in the forest. It would only take them a few hours to get there, so they didn't stop to rest or relax until they did.

The trees were dense, and the air was muggy. The canopy above their heads filtered most of the sunlight, leaving a green haze in the air in front of them. However, each breath was filled with fresh forest air and carried the sweet smell of pine into their noses.

They pressed onward, weaving through the trees and carving a path toward the great willow. Junius carried Aria the entire way to save time, and she slept on his shoulder for most of the journey. Just inside of three hours, they found themselves at the base of the great willow.

Its draping branches seemed to stretch out in all directions as they reached for the skies and arched back down to fall toward the soil below. The leaves formed a beautiful array of shades of green, hanging from the branches like ornaments. The trunk of the tree was gargantuan, nearly fifty feet wide at its largest, and its roots swam through the dirt like a dolphin through the surface of the sea.

"This is beautiful, Daddy," Aria said as she admired the branches.

"It truly is," Evonna agreed.

"There, just beneath that root, do you see it?" Junius said as he pointed to a dip in the soil that looked as though it could be a small cave. "That's where we need to go."

Evonna followed Junius toward the small hole. It was only about three feet in diameter, but it was enough to crawl through without having to squeeze. Junius went first, and Aria followed behind with Evonna coming after. The tunnel was short, only about six feet long, before it opened up into a cavernous area just tall enough to stand. However, just on the opposite side of the room, sat a strange-looking passageway.

The object was seven feet tall and only three feet wide. It came to a point at the top and bottom, and was suspended in the air a few inches off the ground. It appeared stable, but small particles of light fell from it in a mesmerizing display that reminded them of a slow snowfall.

"What is that, Daddy?" Aria asked as she pointed toward the portal.

"That's our gateway to a new home," Junius said in awe.

"It is quite beautiful to look at," Evonna noted aloud.

"Apparently, the farther east you go, the more common these things get. Altomir is likely riddled with them out in the wilds," Junius explained. "But we only need this one. Call me an optimist, but whatever world that's on the other side of this one will be a safe haven for people like us."

"I'm nervous," Evonna said as she looked at the portal.

"Me too, love. But imagine what paradise can await us on the other side," Junius assured. "I will go first, if it makes you feel more at ease."

They walked toward the portal and looked at it for a moment. They were scared of taking such a monumental leap into the unknown, but had come too far to back away. Junius inched toward the portal, reached his arm out, and slowly pushed his hand in.

He winced, but was relieved to feel no pain. He then pushed his arm nearly all the way through until his entire arm was inside. He looked back at Evonna and Aria and gave them a nod before he stepped completely into the portal.

"Are you ready?" Evonna asked Aria.

"I'm scared, Mommy," Aria answered.

"Me too, sweetheart, but it's all going to be okay," Evonna comforted.

She took a quick breath to steel her nerves, and she stepped into the portal with Aria held tight in her arms.

Traveling through the portal felt like being hurled through the cosmos. Streaking lights flew past them as they felt like they were moving at incredible speeds. The atmosphere around them was void and silent, but the feeling of movement still churned within them at a nearly nauseating level. Finally, after a few seconds, they snapped to a stop on a strange-looking platform.

The winds seemed to swirl in every direction as the sky above their heads resonated with astral energy, projecting a colorful array of galaxies across the plane. The ground they were on was flat and spread out a hundred feet in every direction before falling into an empty void beneath. Despite the wind appearing capable of ripping everything to pieces with its turbulent forces alone, the air around them was still and peaceful.

"Where are we?" Evonna asked as she looked around.

"Look at the pretty colors, Mommy!" Aria exclaimed.

"You are in the world between worlds," a powerful voice spoke out around them. "I stopped you here."

They snapped their attention to what appeared to be a projection of a man in the center of the platform. He was translucent and resonated a blueish hue. The projection was detailed enough to make out all his features, displaying his handsome looks and pristine-looking armor.

"My name is Mathius, I am the Overseer of Paxanthus, the world you just attempted to enter. I rule over the world and take care of my people to the fullest extent of my abilities," he explained.

"It's wonderful to meet you, Mathius," Junius said with a respectful bow. "And it's so great to hear you care for your people."

"Who are you, and why have you tried to enter Paxanthus?" Mathius asked.

"My name is Junius, Junius Wildheart. This is my wife, Evonna, and daughter, Aria. We have come to Paxanthus seeking refuge. Our home is in danger, and we have nowhere else to turn to. We just want to live free of harm, and we're so happy to hear about Paxanthus," Junius explained.

"I'm sorry, but you cannot come to Paxanthus," Mathius said bluntly.

"Wait, what? What do you mean? Why not?" Junius asked as he started to breathe heavily.

"I have forbidden the passage of outsiders into Paxanthus, for the safety of my people," Mathius said, his expression saddened.

"Please, Mathius, I beg you. We have nowhere else to go," Junius pleaded. "W-we are great farmers, we can grow your crops. We'll even give you every bit of excess we have to thank you, we just want a safe place to live."

"I'm truly sorry, but I cannot allow it. You are not the first people to come to Paxanthus seeking refuge, and many of these people proved to be much worse than they let on. I assure you, this is nothing personal. But I have to protect my people," Mathius explained.

Junius fell to his knees and placed his hands together, begging, "Please, Mathius. Please. We are desperate. Our home could be overrun by bandits any day now, and I just want my family safe. You can keep me in chains if it helps, however long it takes to prove I am not a threat to your people. I don't even know how to wield a sword."

"Again, I'm sorry, but I cannot allow you to pass through," Mathius denied.

"Then please allow my wife and daughter to come. They are no threat to anyone," Junius begged with tears in his eyes.

"No, Junius, we stay with you no matter where we go," Evonna dismissed.

Mathius sighed before he held his hand out. Almost instantly, a portal identical to the one they went through appeared in front of him. He looked at them with saddened eyes and motioned for them to step through.

"This will take you back to where you came. Please do not try to return again," Mathius instructed. "I wish you all the best, but I must do what's right for my people."

"You would turn us away without remorse?" Junius said as he started to grow angry. "You won't even give us a chance?"

"Tell me, if a stranger approached your door and asked for a place to stay, would you allow him to sleep in the same home as those you love?" Mathius asked. Junius hesitated for a moment, and then hung his head in defeat as Mathius continued, "I take no pride nor feel any pleasure in turning you away, and I hope nothing happens to you or your family. But I am also looking out for those I love, and I do what I must to keep them safe. I hope you understand."

"If not here, can you send us to another world where we can be safe?" Junius asked.

"I'm afraid I don't have the power to do that. I can only control the passage of travel through this gateway alone," Mathius responded. "If there were an alternative where we both benefited, I promise I would take it."

"Let's go, love," Evonna said as she tugged at Junius' shoulder.

"Damn you, Mathius," Junius said in frustration.

"Again, I'm sorry," Mathius said with a sincere but firm tone.

"We'll find somewhere else," Evonna said proudly.

Junius stood to his feet and looked at Mathius in angry disbelief. He couldn't understand why he wouldn't even give them a chance. He knew there was nothing he could do. Mathius was nothing but a projection, so he couldn't fight him. Even if he could, he knew he wouldn't win. After a cold stare, Evonna took Junius' hand and guided them back through the portal to Altomir.

Chapter 4

They stepped back out through the other side in the same place they departed from. From what they could see, it seemed to be the same time of day as it was when they left, so they didn't lose a noticeable amount of time on their trip.

"I can't believe that bastard would turn us away," Junius growled.

"We don't need him or his world," Evonna said, encouraging her husband. "We will find somewhere else."

"You're right," Junius said as he took a deep breath and let it out slowly.

"Aren't I always?" Evonna said with a comforting smile. "We can find somewhere here on Altomir. We don't have to flee our world to find safety."

Junius thought for a while before his eyes lit up and he said, "I have an idea."

"What is it?" Evonna questioned.

"I can take anything we have that may be worth something and carry it into town. I'll trade and sell it all to get food and supplies for long-distance travel on the road. We can head east, away from the Clan of Phantoms, and hopefully find somewhere they'll never reach," Junius suggested.

"Do you think that would work?" Evonna asked.

"Yes, I can even try to barter for our land. Maybe someone in Coniston will want some farmland to use. We could get plenty of food, lamp oil, warm clothing, and other essential supplies. It would be more than enough to get us far away from here," Junius explained.

"What if we run into another dangerous group?" Evonna asked.

"Then we will have some truly awful luck. Hopefully, we don't. We may only be delaying the inevitable this way, but if it means Aria gets to grow up in peace, and you get to sleep soundly, then I'm willing to gamble," Junius replied.

"Okay, dear," Evonna agreed. "We will do what we must. How will we get through the forest?"

"We won't," Junius responded. "We can take Ippy and travel north around the forest. It will be a longer trip, but it means we can carry more gear and food in the wagon."

"Then let's get home and see what we can gather," Evonna agreed. "We should be able to make it back well before sundown."

Junius looked at Evonna with a slight smirk. He admired her courage, her support, and her composure. Despite what he was suggesting, she seemed unfazed by the life-altering decision. She kept him together, and her strength only fueled his passion.

"What is it?" Evonna asked, looking at him curiously.

"I just love you, so much," Junius answered.

"I love you too, dear," Evonna added.

Junius gave her a quick kiss before leading them back through the small tunnel. Once outside, they began their trip back home, through the trees and over huge roots. They followed the same path backward and soon found themselves walking across their fields.

Once they returned home, they began to look through their belongings for anything of value. They looked through their equipment, clothes, belongings, food, and anything else they thought someone might want. They loaded all of it onto the wagon and had it filled to the brim before sundown.

Junius threw the harness on Ippy and attached him to the wagon again as Evonna put together a quick meal for them all to eat before he left. He planned to go immediately to get as far away as fast as possible. He wanted to put distance between them and the Clan of Phantoms as soon as he could, so he needed to get to town to sell. After they had eaten their meal, Junius was standing by the wagon as Evonna and Aria were giving their goodbyes.

"You're leaving again, Daddy?" Aria asked.

"Yes, sweetheart," Junius responded as he hugged her. As he let go, he tapped her on the nose and said, "But guess what?"

"What?" Aria asked curiously.

"This will be the last time," Junius answered. "Once I come back, I'll never have to go to town like this again."

"Really? Never again?" Aria said excitedly. "Hurry back home then, Daddy! I love you!"

"Of course I will, and I love you, too," Junius said with a smile. He stood tall and matched eyes with Evonna before saying, "I'll move as quickly as I can."

"I know you will," Evonna said.

"I love you, more than anything in the world," Junius stated.

"I love, too, dear," Evonna replied. "Now go, the sunset already has a headstart."

Junius smiled and jumped onto the wagon. He gave them a final smile of happiness before he turned his attention to the road ahead of him and mushed Ippy along. Evonna and Aria watched as he faded into the distance before returning inside and winding down for the evening.

The sun set slowly over the horizon as the sounds of wheels turning and hooves stamping the ground repeated in his ears like a record player set to loop. He lost himself in thought about why Mathius would turn them away like that, and why he wouldn't just listen to them, or give them a chance. It bugged him, but he knew there was nothing he could do about it, so he tried to refocus his thoughts on what he could change instead.

He wondered what awaited them on the other side of the forest. Was it just like here? Were there other criminal organizations? Were there safe havens for good people? All kinds of thoughts swirled through his mind, which helped pass the time as he traveled. A mix of excitement, worry, and hope fueled these thoughts, and the days felt like nothing more than a few moments as he trotted toward Coniston for the last time.

Once he could see the town on the horizon, a strange feeling welled up in the pit of his stomach. He kept a sharp eye out for any signs of the Clan of Phantoms, but was relieved to find the roads between him and his destination were empty.

He strolled into town to the surprise of a few and made his way to his usual spot to set up his cart. He spoke with some of the locals and informed them that he had many goods to sell, most of which weren't produce. He asked them to spread the word, as he needed to sell as much as he could.

The townsfolk trickled in a little at a time and bartered with Junius. They offered him many things, but he only agreed to trade for gold or survival supplies. This led to him collecting more gold than anything else, but that was okay with him. He could use the gold to buy some supplies after he finished selling. Eventually, Bradley caught wind of Junius being in town and made his way over.

"Junius, I thought you were leaving," Bradley said with confusion.

"I tried," Junius responded.

"What happened?" Bradley asked.

"We were turned away. The portal went to a world called Paxanthus, but the leader of that world told us we couldn't enter. He stopped us before we ever set foot there, and wouldn't listen to my pleas. We had to come back," Junius explained.

"I'm so sorry, Junius. Had I known, I wouldn't have suggested it," Bradley apologized.

"It's not your fault, Bradley. I appreciate you trying to help us," Junius assured.

"Is that why you're here, selling all your worldly possessions? What will you do now?" Bradley asked.

"Yeah, we're going to pack up and head east, around the eastern forest, and see what's on the other side," Junius answered. "You should come too. You can bring your family, and we can all travel together."

"Junius, I've already told you, I'm too old for all that. Besides, I could never convince the missus," Bradley said with a laugh. "We'll get by right here, don't worry about us."

"Okay, if you say so," Junius dismissed. "I'm almost done here, then I'll be heading back. I'll stop by and say goodbye before I go."

"Sounds good," Bradley said with a wave as he walked away.

Junius waved back and shook his head. He knew Bradley was a stubborn old fool, but he didn't think he was that stuck in his roots. He continued to sell everything he had, and it all went surprisingly quickly. He wasn't expecting to sell everything, but as sure as the sun would rise in the morning, he did. He had a few items in his cart: some rope, rations, and a tinderbox. But, most of what he gained was gold.

He didn't take the time to count what he had earned, but he knew it was more gold than he had ever seen in one place in his entire life. He planned to visit the other shops and purchase goods for their journey, and decided to start at Bradley's butchery. He figured a good dinner would be optimal before they started on their journey.

He tied off Ippy and grabbed enough coin to purchase a slab of meat before tucking away the rest of the gold and securing his wagon. After that, he walked around the corner toward the butchery, but something wasn't right. He could hear someone yelling in the distance, and saw a few people running around the corner. At first, he thought it may have been a scuffle breaking out, but when he turned the corner, he immediately saw everything.

He witnessed one of the bandits from the Clan of Phantoms standing in the middle of the road. The bandit was bloodied and looked like he had been hit a few times, but otherwise, he was okay. He held a knife in his hand and had someone on the ground on the road. Junius stopped in his tracks once he saw them, but it took some people shuffling around before he saw who was on the ground; it was his friend Bradley.

Junius' heart started to race, and his mind began to tear at him. He wanted to rush in and help his friend, but he didn't want to get into a fight. He knew fighting would only lead to him getting hurt. He froze in fear and indecisiveness. He tried to move, but his legs wouldn't allow it. He began to breathe heavily as he watched everything happen.

The bandit took a few breaths before leaning down and grabbing Bradley by the hair. He pulled him up to his knees and smashed a punch into the side of his head. Bradley's face was a bloody mess, and he was bleeding from multiple cuts around his eyes and cheeks. It looked like he had been beaten badly. The bandit pressed his blade against Bradley's throat in preparation to cut him open.

That's when the bandit looked out at everyone else standing in the road and shouted, "Let this be a lesson to anyone foolish enough to resist the Clan of Phantoms. We take what we want and we do what we want. Our word is law, and breaking the law is punishable by death."

Before anyone could respond, the bandit drug his blade across Bradley's throat and sliced him open. Blood poured from the wound immediately and started to saturate his shirt with red. Bradley looked as though he was trying to breathe, but his airway was filled, and nothing but blood entered his lungs. Within seconds, Bradley fell to the ground and bled to death in the street.

Junius' heart sank into his stomach. He couldn't believe what he was seeing. He never imagined Bradley would be targeted, and he had no idea why they would do what they did. In his moment of panic, the only thing he could do was flee. He turned and ran back to his wagon as fast as he could. He tossed the bag of gold into the back of the wagon and untied Ippy. He jumped on and mushed Ippy back out of town as fast as the old horse would take him. He was panicked and didn't know what else to do except get as far away from Coniston as possible. He would never return.

Ippy moved as fast as his old legs would take him for miles. Eventually, the old stallion couldn't pull the wagon any further and collapsed on the road. Junius jumped down to check on him and immediately could tell he had pushed him too hard. He looked around frantically to see if anyone was around, but he was alone. There were only a couple of hours of daylight left, so Junius decided he would let Ippy rest and continue sometime after nightfall.

"I'm sorry, old buddy," Junius said as he patted Ippy on the head. "We just needed to get away from there as fast as possible. Take a few minutes, you've earned some rest."

He sat down next to Ippy and rested his head back against the horse. He listened to his heartbeat and breathing, trying to distract himself from everything that had just happened. Bradley was dead, his good friend, and he had no idea why. Also, it was clear the Clan of Phantoms was acting in full force already, meaning there was no more time to prepare.

He wondered what would happen to Coniston now that they had fully taken over. He also wondered if the towns to the north were all captured. He didn't get a chance to buy anything, so he had ample gold to spend, and going back wasn't an option. He thought about where he could go as he listened to Ippy's breathing, wondering what all they would need, and how long it would take them to get where they needed to go.

As he lost himself in thought, the sun began to set. He did his best to calm his nerves, but more than ever, he was ready to put distance between himself and the bandits that threatened the region. As he swirled in his own mind, the breathing of Ippy acted like a lullaby, and he unintentionally drifted off to sleep.

Junius began to stir in the early morning hours. He didn't realize he had fallen asleep for the first few moments, but once it dawned on him, he snapped awake. His eyes shot open, and he quickly sat up, but his heart sank into his stomach as soon as he did. He looked around to see that he wasn't alone.

Four men, the same men who had robbed him before, were standing near him. One of them looked down on him with a menacing grin while the others had pulled everything he had out of his wagon and scattered it all around the road. Junius noticed what was going on and immediately began to panic internally.

"You've got quite the stash of gold here, friend," One of the bandits said as he knelt next to him. "What do you think you're doing with all of that?"

"I was using it for supplies," Junius answered.

"But you're heading the opposite way from town. What's up this way?" the bandit asked.

"I was considering going to Woodpine. Coniston didn't have everything I needed, and I didn't want to burden my horse unnecessarily. I know Woodpine has an ample supply of goods," Junius replied, coming up with a believable lie as fast as possible.

"You're right, you do have an old ass horse," the bandit agreed. We should lighten his load more. We'll take that heavy gold off your hands so you don't have to stress the old boy."

A lump grew in Junius' throat, and anger welled up inside of him. He clenched his jaw in frustration, but knew he couldn't stop them. All four of them were armed, and he had no fighting experience.

The bandit looked at him and laughed as he could see Junius' anger. He teased, "Aww, does that make you mad? Do you wanna hit me? You wanna stop us from taking your gold?"

"I couldn't, even if I wanted to," Junius mumbled angrily.

"You're damn right you couldn't," the bandit stated as he stood to his feet. He turned to the others and shouted, "Take all the gold and… Actually, take everything."

Junius' eyes shot up as he blurted, "Wait, please, no! Take the gold, but I need the rest of those supplies. They're useless to you guys anyway."

"No one asked you, now shut your mouth," the bandit growled.

"Please, I'm begging you. We need those supplies," Junius pleaded.

"I said shut your damn mouth!" the bandit snapped as he slammed a punch into Junius' face.

Junius fell to the side, his cheek throbbing from the strike, but a rage washed across him that seemed to smother any rational thought. He pushed himself to his feet and jumped at the bandit, landing a punch of his own.

"Oh hell, this one has some balls," one of the other bandits said with a laugh.

"Stay back for a second, I'm going to enjoy this," the bandit Junius hit ordered.

Junius followed up with another swing, but this time the bandit ducked underneath. Junius stumbled and was crushed hard with an uppercut that snapped his head backward. The bandit then smashed a punch into his stomach, grabbed him by the back of the head, slammed another punch into his nose, pulled his head downward, crushed a knee into his face, lifted another hard punch into his stomach, pushed him backward, and kicked him in the chest to knock him to the ground.

"Get up," the bandit grunted.

Junius throbbed in pain already. He could feel his face swelling and blood falling down his cheek. He placed his hands underneath himself and started to push off the ground when he felt a thunderous kick blast him in the side of the head.

"I said get up, you pathetic bastard," the bandit taunted.

Junius tried to push himself up again, but this time he felt a kick to his ribs from the opposite side. He winced in pain as the crackling of bone rang in his ear. He then felt a boot crush into the back of his head, bouncing his skull off the dirt. What followed was nothing short of torture. The four bandits proceeded to beat Junius within an inch of his life. They kicked, punched, and spat on his body long after he started to lose consciousness. Junius tried to get back to his feet multiple times, but the damage was too great.

He eventually fell to the ground in a swollen, bloody heap as they continued to attack him. He was sure he was going to die. The last thing he heard before his vision faded to black was the bandits laughing at his agony as his body started to feel numb.

Chapter 5

The feeling of his ribs grinding with each shallow breath slowly crept to the forefront of his mind. The pain from the rest of his injuries became more noticeable a little at a time, and eventually, he opened his eyes to see nothing but dirt.

He groaned in pain. His face was swollen, and he could barely open his left eye. His ribs were broken on both sides, and breathing was agonizing. His arms felt weak and shaky, and he guessed his right forearm might have been broken as well. He had never been in this much pain before in his life, and it was unbearable.

After a moment, he tried to put his arms underneath himself and push himself up off the ground. He struggled at first, but eventually he was able to pull his knees underneath and sit up on his feet. He grimaced in pain and felt like he was going to faint, but held himself together.

After he sat up, he looked around and nearly cried. The bandits destroyed his wagon, leaving it in pieces. They took everything he had except for a bundle of rope, and they killed Ippy. The horse had multiple stab wounds, but couldn't run away because he was strapped to the broken wagon.

Junius began to sob as he looked around. It felt like his entire world was falling apart, and there was nothing he could do about it. He felt stupid for ever fighting back, and wondered what had come over him. There was no chance he could have won that fight, and he knew it. And now he was devastated with injuries and losing his horse.

He painstakingly made his way up to his feet, as he knew there was no choice but to walk. He grabbed the rope that was left, hung it across his chest like the strap of a satchel, and started limping toward his home. He estimated he could make it home around nightfall, and he was terrified to break the news to Evonna. He lost it all, and it was all his fault. If he hadn't made Ippy run for so long, he could have made it farther and out of harm's way. If he hadn't fallen asleep, they never would have caught up to him. If he hadn't fought back, Ippy might still be alive, and he wouldn't be in so much pain. If he had listened to Evonna and not wasted an entire day trying to leave through the portal, they might have had a day's headstart on all of this.

These thoughts raced through his head as tears fell from his eyes. He just wanted to be home and rest. He wanted to hug Evonna and see Aria. No matter how much pain he was in, his family could make everything alright, so he pressed onward.

For hours, Junius limped with one leg after the other until he hit the final stretch to his home. The sun was already disappearing behind the horizon, but he would make it back before nightfall. His body was heavy, and his legs felt weak. Each step was more difficult than the last, and walking for so long was brutally painful. His head hung as he stared at the ground, but he was going to be okay. He would heal his injuries for a few days, and they would be able to leave after about a week. They could still get to safety, even without proper supplies.

As the dirt passed underneath him, something caught his eye that he wasn't expecting. Stamped into the ground beneath his feet was a boot print. His eyes widened as he looked around and saw multiple tracks, all of which were aimed toward his home. He quickly started to shuffle as fast as he could until he reached the next hill and was able to see his house.

His heart beat so heavily he could feel it in his neck, it thumped in his ears as he nearly fell to the ground from stumbling over his injured feet. His adrenaline was spiked as he forced his body forward and up the incline. As his head crested the top of the hill, his worst nightmare sat in front of him. In the distance, he could see that his home had been burned to the ground. His fields had been torched, and everything was destroyed.

"Oh no. No, no, no, no, no," Junius muttered to himself as his lip began to quiver and his breathing grew rapid and more shallow. "This can't be happening. Please, God, this can't be true."

He broke into a jog and started moving as fast as he could. He didn't care about his injuries, his home, his goods, or anything else. The only thing going through his mind was his wife and daughter. He couldn't bear the thought of anything happening to them, and just wanted to see that they were okay. He ran and didn't slow down, his heart pumping as fast as it could to fuel his aching limbs, until he finally reached the edge of his farmstead.

He looked around in horror at all the destruction. Nothing was left standing except the charred support beams of his home. The walls were gone, the roof caved in, and the rubble sat crumpled within. He could barely breathe as he ran toward his house. He struggled to see through teary eyes as he started to move rubble away, and his chest began to heave after he lifted what remained of one of his walls.

"Please, no. Please… please let this be a bad dream," Junius whispered to himself.

He dropped to his knees and broke down in anguish as he slowly reached out and touched the charred remains of small feet bound in burnt rope. His hands trembled as he grazed his fingertips over the remains. He knew it was his daughter; He knew it was Aria.

"Please wake up!" Junius cried as he hit himself in the thigh. "Wake up, you bastard… You sick bastard."

He crawled over to his daughter and reached down to her. He slowly pulled her close to him and held her to his chest as his heart shattered into pieces. He cried out in pain as he rocked back and forth on his knees. He didn't know what to do.

"Please, no. This can't be happening," Junius muttered as he looked down at Aria through teary eyes. "Please wake up, please."

He began to wail in misery as he looked around the rest of his home. He couldn't take the pressure that squeezed at his chest. It felt like his heart was going to burst as his entire life came crashing down around him. It was too much to bear.

"Why?" Junius shouted out between his sobbing. "Why is this happening? What did we do to deserve this? She was only four! They didn't do anything… Why gods? Why do this to them?"

That's when he saw the most haunting thing imaginable. From underneath another collapsed wall was Evonna. Her body was just as burnt as Aria's, but her eyes still looked the same. It looked like she was staring at Junius from beyond the mortal realm, and he found it hard to breathe as soon as he saw her.

"No, gods no. I'm so sorry, Evonna," Junius cried as he looked into his wife's eyes. "I should have been here. I shouldn't have left. I am so sorry. I'm so, so sorry."

Junius gently laid his daughter down on the ground before crawling over to his wife's remains. He pulled the rubble from atop her body and pushed it to the side. The heat from the crumbled building was barely noticeable as Junius' mind reeled in torment. He placed his forehead against Evonna's chest as he cried uncontrollably.

He had nothing left. No home, no goods, no plan, no family, and no reason to live. Everything he ever cared about was stripped from him in an instant, and he wasn't granted the fortune of dying with them. His mind fractured, and his body trembled in pain. He was numb to the wounds he suffered, but the relentless agony of his new reality tore at every fiber of his being. He didn't want to feel the pain anymore. He didn't want to feel anything at all.

He sat back on his feet, his cheeks were covered in tears as they fell from his eyes and dripped from the bottom of his chin. His breathing was rapid and shallow, and his heart raced in his chest. He couldn't take it anymore… he wanted to die.

As the harrowing reality clawed deeper into his psyche, he felt like a husk. He couldn't take the pain, the devastating, torturous pain that ripped at his insides like a monster clawing its way inside of him. He wanted to escape. He wanted to be with his wife and daughter. He wanted to join them in a world far from here and wipe this memory from existence. He wanted death.

"How could they do this?" Junius thought to himself, trying to make sense of the torture he felt. "Why would they hurt a woman and child? Why would they take their lives?"

He felt numb as he looked down at his chest. The bundle of rope still sat wrapped across his body, and he slowly raised his hand to pull it off. He held the rope in his hands as his mind locked onto the only solution he could think of. He was going to kill himself.

He looked around at the husk of his home and noticed some of the support beams were still standing. He found one that wasn't too hard to reach, and made up his mind. He stood to his feet and started to look for some solid pieces of rubble to stack just high enough for him to reach the beam. The platform he made was wobbly, but he didn't care. He climbed up the short platform and found himself eye-to-eye with the support beam.

Junius looked down to see that he was only a few feet off the ground. He then laid the rope over the beam and started to fasten it securely, ensuring it wouldn't slip under tension. Once the rope was securely bound, he grabbed the other end and felt panic growing in his gut. He slowly raised the rope to his neck and started to tie it behind him. His eyes were wide as he fashioned the slipknot and knew he only had one thing left to do.

The platform beneath his feet was wobbly already, and he teetered back and forth as he looked down at his feet. The ground had never seemed so far away. His vision blurred as he looked directly at his grave. He didn't want to die, but he didn't want to live in a world without his family. He loved them more than himself, and to him, there was no reason to keep going without them.

He took a deep breath; he didn't know why he did, maybe it was instinctual. He knew the moment the rope was tight, it would break his neck, and no amount of air would prolong that. As he exhaled slowly, he knew it was time.

"Please forgive me, Evonna, but I can't do this without you," Junius whispered.

In a quick motion, he kicked the platform away and watched it tumble to the ground. Everything seemed to be happening in slow motion as he felt his body immediately falling toward the floor. It was almost comforting to know it was over. No matter his thoughts, it was too late to go back. All his pain would be over in a flash, and he could be with his family once again. As soon as he felt the rope beginning to tighten around his neck, his lip quivered in relief, and he felt the rope snap tight, and his eyes closed.

A warm rush shot across his body as the rope constricted around his neck. He just wanted it to be over, but for some reason, it felt like it was taking an eternity for such a brief moment in time to pass. That's when he heard the break and felt his soul start to free-fall into the abyss. He plummeted into darkness, falling for what felt like an eternity until finally he felt a crash as his soul ground to a halt.

He paused for a moment, but felt confused. Why did death feel so similar? Why didn't he hear the singing of angels? Or why weren't there flames of hell spouting around him? Why wasn't his family greeting him? Why was he still in so much pain? Why was he still broken?

He slowly opened his eyes, hoping to see his family's faces. He just wanted to hear their voices. He wanted to hear that everything would be okay now. But he realized he wasn't dead. He was lying on the floor of his home with a rope only slightly constricting his neck. His vision was still hazy, but he looked up at the beam the rope was tied to and saw that the rope was still there. Then he looked farther down and realized what had happened.

Instead of the rope breaking his neck like he wanted, the snapping sound he heard was the rope itself breaking into two. The defeat he felt was only compounded by his failure to kill himself. His failures cost him everything he ever cared about, but he couldn't even take his own life. His hollow soul was forced to live another moment in this torturous existence.

He sat up and reluctantly pulled the rope from his neck. He was in shock, and the tears had stopped. He was prepared to die, but when that failed, it sent him reeling. He could barely breathe, and his hands trembled. He couldn't form any rational thoughts, and his mind felt like it had fractured into pieces. He didn't know what to do. He slowly stood to his feet and began to shamble away. He didn't move with any purpose; he had no destination; he just moved. His legs, still throbbing in pain, stepped one after the other without his input. It was like his body was on autopilot, and he was sitting in the farthest corner of his subconscious, trying to escape the reality of what was happening.

He walked toward the forest mindlessly. Stumbling every few steps, but pressing onward. He kept walking until he was inside the forest, and then started to snake and weave through the trees. He still didn't know what he was doing, but he didn't care. In the depths of his mind, he still wanted to die, but he didn't have the strength to try again himself.

As he pushed aside branches and fell over the mangled roots of grove trees, he waited patiently. He figured something in the wilds would have to be hungry, and guessed that it was only a matter of time before a predator came along and ate him. Would it be a tiger? A bear? Some unknown monster lurking deep within the forest? He didn't care; he just wanted it to be over with.

He continued to walk for hours. The aching of his injuries returned to the forefront of his attention as the adrenaline faded from his body. He was overwhelmed with grief, so every movement was sluggish and felt clunky. He kept walking until the sun disappeared from the sky and the forest became so dark he couldn't see what was in front of him.

"This is it," he thought to himself. "This is where I die."

He fell to his knees and then over on his side. It was cold, and the ground was unforgivingly uncomfortable, but he couldn't see well enough to move, and he didn't care. He tried to sleep; he wanted to put his consciousness away in hopes that it would hurry his inevitable death, but he couldn't. His physical pain wouldn't allow him to fall asleep, but his mental pain made him want nothing more than to disconnect.

As he lay there in the dark, all he could see was Evonna's face. The ghostly blank stare of her eyes clawed at his mind. It didn't matter if he closed his eyes or left them open; the oppressive darkness wouldn't allow him to look at anything else. He was forced to relive the imagery of the most haunting thing he had ever seen, over and over, playing on a loop. This persisted throughout the night.

The sun started to peek through the canopy of the forest, giving Junius a glimpse of the world around him and finally granting him a slight reprieve from his mental anguish. The hours of the night before ticked by slowly, but no matter how hard he tried, Junius couldn't fall asleep.

After the sun created enough brightness for him to
make out his environment, Junius decided to keep moving. He
couldn't stand to lie still anymore; he needed to get his mind
distracted enough to numb the pain, so he started walking
eastward once again. The fact that nothing picked him for a
free meal was disappointingly surprising to him.

The air was thick and humid as he marched deeper
through the dense trees. The sound of bugs and birds filled his
ears, and he could feel sweat dripping down his arms and
falling from his fingertips. His vision tunneled directly ahead of
him, but he still had no destination. He just wanted to keep
moving.

His body was in incredible pain. He was covered in
cuts and bruises, and every breath he took felt like a knife
stabbing into his lungs. He estimated that six of his ribs were
broken, and his forearm felt worse than before, so he was sure
that he had at least a small break. Each step felt like lifting
sandbags as his tired body ached in pain.

He hadn't eaten or drunk anything in over a day at this
point, and fatigue was starting to wear him down. He
wondered how long it took to die from a lack of water, as he
was sweating profusely, and putting nothing back. He knew his
body had to be running itself ragged trying to repair the
damage done under these conditions.

The hours ticked by slowly, each one feeling like a
lifetime of emptiness. He wasn't sure how far he had made it,
but he had no idea where he was. He looked up and saw the
sun was at the peak of its path through the sky, so he
assumed he had made it around twenty miles since he started
walking.

Junius kept his body in motion as he lost himself in thought. He dwelled on all the possibilities had he done anything differently. Dozens of points in the days leading up to the moment he found his family could have been changed, and likely would mean they were still alive. The despair it brought him was soul-crushing to know that his choices had led to his family being killed. It corroded his soul.

Before long, Junius noticed his feet were barely moving. His legs had grown too weak to step a full stride, and his arms were like dead weights down by his side. In his dissociative state, he failed to realize just how deathly exhausted he had become. He was delirious, his vision was fading slowly, and he just wanted to lie down somewhere.

He looked around and saw a small cave entrance that led into a rock face just a few hundred feet away. He figured that was the best place to lie down. He chose that to be his final resting place. He shambled toward the entrance, taking much longer to get there than was usually necessary, and ran his hand along the stone wall as he stepped inside.

The floor was cool; he could feel it underneath his feet, which was a nice contrast to the heat outside. However, comfort wasn't on his mind; he just wanted to close his eyes. He had been going for nearly two full days in awful condition. His feet were swollen, his body battered, and his mind was fractured. Finally, after all the miles he walked, he was ready to close his eyes.

Unlike the night before, his body was incredibly weakened due to a lack of nutrition and hydration. His eyes wanted to close before he even made it to the cave, so he knew he would be able to sleep. He was desperate to lie down and drift off into nothingness. He was desperate to die.

He walked into the cave far enough to get away from the entrance before he finally collapsed to the ground. His legs were too weak to crouch, and his arms were too weak to catch himself. His face slammed into the stone floor, cutting open his cheek immediately. He could feel the warmth of his blood as it started to pool around his face, but he didn't move. He just closed his eyes as he felt his body failing. It was finally time to go. It was time to be with his family and beg for their forgiveness. He hoped they still loved him, even after the pain he brought them. He hoped they were waiting for him.

Chapter 6

The blackness of death wasn't like Junius expected it to be. He drifted through an endless void, but there was nothing else. No hell, no heaven, no angels, no demons, and no family; just all-consuming blackness. He tried to swim through it, but nothing moved. No matter how much he tried, his body stayed motionless. He felt like he drifted for weeks, lost in the void of limbo, doomed to suffer an eternity in isolation, a punishment for his failings as a husband and father.

Suddenly, the silent void was interrupted by the slightest sound of crackling. At first, it was faint, but eventually grew louder until it finally sounded like the light crackling of a campfire. Then the feeling of warmth crept into the void. It felt like a warm blanket was draped across his entire body, especially his face. It was oddly soothing. Then, he was sure he could smell burning wood.

Then the soothing feeling quickly spiraled into a nightmare. Suddenly, he was standing at the edge of his farmstead and looking at his house in flames. His pain was gone, and the injuries to his body were non-existent. But he could hear the crackling wood beginning to crumble under the oppressive flames, and the heat from the inferno washed over his skin. He quickly ran toward his house, looking for Evonna and Aria, but they weren't around.

That's when he heard screaming from inside the house. He frantically sprinted toward his home and didn't hesitate to rush headfirst into the blaze. He could barely see through the thick smoke, but it didn't matter. Getting his family out was all he could think about.

"Where are you!" Junius shouted as he tried to scan through the smoke.

No matter where he searched, the screams of his family always seemed to be coming from outside his field of view. They were starting to weaken and growing increasingly difficult to hear as the seconds ticked by.

"Evonna! Aria! Please answer me!" Junius shouted desperately as he started to crawl through his home.

Finally, he spotted them. Aria was already lying motionless on the ground, but Evonna was moving. He quickly crawled toward them and reached out to grab Evonna's hand.

"We have to get out of here," Junius insisted as he started to pull.

"My legs are stuck," Evonna said in pain.

Junius quickly slid over and tried to pull the rubble from atop his wife, but it was no use. No matter how hard he pulled, the beam wouldn't budge.

"Evonna, you have to help me," Junius pleaded.

"Why?" Evonna said ominously.

Junius looked down at her and was frightened, stumbling away from her. Her eyes were as black as midnight, and her face was expressionless.

"Why would I help you? You didn't help us." Evonna asked with a hollowed voice.

"Evonna, I know I messed up, but I'm here now, please help me get you free," Junius begged.

"Look at Aria, Junius, she's already dead," Evonna said coldly.

Junius looked down at his daughter, and she wasn't moving. Her feet and hands were bound exactly as they were when he found her. The pain stabbed him in the heart just as it did before as he looked at his child lying motionless on the ground.

"You see? You're already too late, Junius. Where were you?" Evonna asked.

"I was trying to get here as fast as I could," Junius said with a shaky voice. "I was moving as fast as my legs would take me, I promise... I tried."

"But that wasn't fast enough, was it?" Evonna asked. "You weren't strong enough. You weren't there when we needed you, Junius."

"I tried," Junius cried. "I didn't know this was happening... I didn't know."

"You failed us. We're dead because of you," Evonna said as her voice trailed off and her eyes changed back.

Junius looked at her and saw the same haunting expression she had before as his heart beat out of his chest. The flames began to close in around him and wash over their bodies. The heat was excruciating, but his skin wouldn't burn. His stomach turned, his head throbbed, and his heart ripped to shreds as he looked at his family, but for some reason, he couldn't burn with them.

Suddenly, his eyes shot open as he sat up abruptly. The pain returned to his body from the numerous injuries he felt, but something was different. He looked down at his arm and saw it was splinted with a few straight sticks and some vines. He saw he was covered with a warm robe and was lying on a bed of leaves.

"Easy, you haven't had time to heal," a voice spoke out from next to him.

Junius quickly snapped his attention to his left and saw an elven man right beside him, warming his hands by a campfire. The man looked like a scholar, but his clothes were dirtier than a typical scholar's would be. Junius' eyes were wide as he tried to understand what was going on, but he had no clue. He was still in the same cave he stumbled into, but he was in better condition than before.

"You should lie back down," the man suggested. "You were in bad shape."

"Who are you?" Junius asked.

"My name is Ehrindil. And yours?" he asked.

"I'm... Junius," he answered hesitantly. "What did you do?"

"Well, I was out looking for supplies when I saw you stumble into this cave. By the time I was able to follow you in here, you had already passed out. I tried to wake you up, but once that didn't work, I decided to pull you back from death's grip," Ehrindil explained triumphantly.

"Why?" Junius asked, with tears in his eyes. "Why did you do that? You should have just let me die. I was almost with them again…"

Ehrindil looked at him, confused for a moment before the dots started to connect. His expression shifted as he said, "I didn't know that was your intention. I don't know who you lost, but I'm sorry you lost them. I'll be honest, even if I did know, I wouldn't have let you die."

"Why not? Junius asked angrily. "Why would you insist on someone you don't know living when they want to die?"

"Because death won't end your grief. It will do nothing but prolong it. You will carry that grief with you into the afterlife and shoulder that burden for an eternity. No, if I did know what you were going through, I would have made doubly sure you had a chance to redeem your pain," Ehrindil elaborated.

"I don't understand," Junius stated. "Why do you care so much about a stranger?"

"Because there are plenty of people who don't," Ehrindil answered. "It's only right that I try to counter just a fraction of that."

Junius soaked in his words. He was still confused about who this man was, why he was there, and why he looked like a disheveled nobleman. He appreciated his kindness, but was still skeptical of the entire situation. He wondered if he was still dreaming, but everything around him felt real enough.

"Who even are you?" Junius asked. "Not just your name, who are you really?"

"As in what am I doing out in the middle of the woods scraping together crumbs to get by?" Ehrindil asked.

"Sure, yeah," Junius answered.

"I could ask you the same thing," Ehrindil replied.

"You already know why I'm out here," Junius rebutted.

"Not the particulars," Ehrindil said with one eyebrow raised.

"You first," Junius said, dismissing his attempts to learn more.

"Fair," Ehrindil responded. "I'm a scholar, amateur practitioner of the arcane, and a seeker of knowledge. I strive to learn as much as possible in the time I have left to live, no matter how long or short that may be."

"And you plan on learning out here in the wilds?" Junius asked.

"Well, no. I am out here seeking refuge, currently. You see, I'm not from your world. Altomir is a foreign realm to me, and I came here through less than intelligent means. I am keeping myself out of the spotlight until my friend comes to get me," Ehrindil answered.

"Your friend?" Junius inquired.

"Yes. I left him a letter stating where I went, though I did leave it in a puzzle box. In hindsight, that wasn't the best idea. He is notoriously awful at puzzles," Ehrindil said, trailing off at the end.

"Ah, so he's like your dumb bodyguard friend?" Junius asked.

"Quite the contrary," Ehrindil responded. "He is arguably more intelligent than I am; he's just bad at solving riddles. It was my only way to tease his intellect and claim any sort of dominance in the category. Quite a fun way to pass the time as well," Ehrindil explained.

"How do you know he will come?" Junius asked.

"He will, I just know it. Then we will go back home and get off this dreadful rock," Ehrindil answered.

"Leave Altomir? You can do that?" Junius asked, his voice tinged with excitement.

However, his expression changed almost immediately. The sole reason he wanted to leave Altomir was to protect his family, and it was too late for that. His head dropped slightly as he let out a long sigh.

"Yes, we will leave once he arrives. You're welcome to come if you'd like. My world is a much more livable place than this one. Do you have anyone you'd want to bring?" Ehrindil asked.

"No," Junius replied softly. "Not anymore."

Ehrindil paused before answering. He had hoped that Junius still had some connection to people around him, but he could tell that wasn't the case. He could see it in Junius' eyes that he was alone.

"Is that who you lost?" Ehrindil asked gently.

"Yeah," Junius answered.

"Do you want to talk about it?" Ehrindil asked, trying to comfort him.

"There isn't much to talk about. I wasn't where I should have been, and now my family is gone. Hell, even if I were there, there would have been nothing I could have done. I'm too weak. But it would have been better to die with them than to live," Junius said as his lip began to quiver.

Ehrindil sat in silence; he didn't know what to say, but he also knew that simply listening was enough. He could see the agony Junius was going through, and wished there was a way to cure him of his pain.

"I would give anything to trade places with them. I would die a million painful deaths if it meant they could keep living. They did nothing wrong and were killed for it. My little girl just turned four. She had so much life left to live, and they took it from her. I just want to hug them one more time," Junius said as he stared blankly. His jaw clenched as he said, "And I would do anything to get back at the bastards who took them from me."

"Who did it?" Ehrindil asked.

"It was the Clan of Phantoms," Junius answered. He remembered that Ehrindil wasn't from Altomir, so he elaborated, "They are a bandit organization that dominates the area I came from. They are ruthless and evil. They take whatever they want and kill whoever tries to stop them. Well, most of the time. They wouldn't grant me death. Instead, they left me barely alive and killed my family instead."

"I'm genuinely sorry to hear. That is awful, and no one should have to go through such a terrible experience," Ehrindil comforted.

"That's why I wanted to die. I have nothing left to live for. Without them, I'm nothing; nobody. I don't know what to do, and I wish you had let me pass on," Junius stated.

"You still have plenty to live for," Ehrindil said. "Your family is watching you as we speak. How do you think they feel hearing you say such things about yourself?"

"What makes you think that?" Junius asked.

"Because that's what I believe. Just like I believe my family watches over me. I don't have a wife or children, but I do have loved ones who were taken too soon. I know they can see me, and I want to make them proud before it's my time to join them. I want to bring stories with me to the afterlife and tell them tales of grand adventures and fascinating finds," Ehrindil clarified. "So don't assume their death is the end for them. Make sure you take a lifetime of stories back to tell them later."

"If you say so," Junius dismissed. He felt his cheek and noticed the cut was completely healed. He asked, "How long have I been out?"

"Three days," Ehrindil responded.

"That couldn't be, I had a pretty bad cut here and it couldn't have healed in three days," Junius argued.

"That was nothing a little magic couldn't fix," Ehrindil replied.

"Magic? You know magic?" Junius asked.

"Of course I do. I said that I am an apprentice of the arcane. I know all sorts of magic, though most of it is surface-level. My friend was better at harnessing the more advanced spells," Ehrindil answered.

"That's amazing. Magic is rare here on Altomir. Anyone who learns how to use it typically will rise through the ranks of a bandit organization and secure a high position. The strongest magic users here are the leaders of those groups," Junius explained.

"Well, I have no interest in that," Ehrindil dismissed. "I am not a fan of conflict anyway, that's why I'm out here in the woods."

"Running from someone?" Junius asked.

"Precisely," Ehrindil agreed.

"So what will you do now?" Junius asked.

"I will spend as many days out here in hiding as necessary until my chance to go home arrives. Until then, I will forage for what food I can and drink from the creek nearby. I made some buckets to hold water, too," Ehrindil said as he pointed to his makeshift tools. "It's not a great living, but it will get me by for now. What about you?"

"I don't know," Junius answered. "I don't know what to do."

"Well, stay here with me," Ehrindil suggested. "Your wounds are still healing, so you have a few weeks before you're back on your feet. Plus, I could use the extra help getting this place more livable. Once my friend arrives, you're welcome to come with me if you'd like. Or you can stay here, but I hope I can convince you to vacate your path of suicide before it's said and done."

Junius looked around the cave, and then at Ehrindil. He was confused as to why this man had gone to such great lengths to help him, but it was oddly comforting to have someone to talk to. It made him feel just a tiny bit better, even if the difference was barely noticeable. He didn't know what he planned to do, or even if he wanted to live, but he figured it wouldn't hurt to stay busy until he figured it out.

"Okay, I'll help," Junius agreed. "What do you need me to do?"

"Nothing just yet," Ehrindil answered. "You still need to heal first. Afterward, we'll figure it out."

"Okay," Junius said as he rested his head back onto the makeshift pillow.

He looked down at his chest and saw the corner of a paper sticking out from inside his chest pocket. He took the paper and opened it, but immediately felt a gripping pain in his chest. It was the drawing that Aria made for him, and it was the only thing he had left of her. He rolled onto his side to face away from Ehrindil as tears streamed down the side of his face, holding the drawing close to his chest. The physical pain he felt was nothing compared to the mental anguish he was going through.

He folded the paper back up and put it back into his pocket. He made a vow to himself to keep the drawing safe and never let anything happen to it. He had already lost everything; he didn't want to lose the last gift he would ever receive as well.

He did his best to rest his mind, though it was far from easy. The company was a distraction, and the conversation helped him think about something other than the memories that plagued him. For the time being, he would do his best to get his mind off things, and helping Ehrindil seemed like the best way to do it.

Chapter 7

The next couple of months passed by slowly. Junius didn't say too much, but he did spend some time listening to Ehrindil and the stories he told. He admired the wild tales, despite assuming that most of them were exaggerated. However, the world of dragons, gold, mysticism, and adventure seemed exciting, and he admired Ehrindil for pursuing a life full of it.

During the first couple of weeks, Ehrindil would periodically use his magic to accelerate Junius' healing. His wounds started to close, and his bones were mending well. Junius was appreciative of the catering, but he began to grow restless just sitting around all the time. The longer he was idle, the more his grief tore at his soul, so he wanted to distract himself.

Despite Ehrindil's recommendations, Junius started to get up and move after a couple of weeks. His body still hurt, and his muscles had grown weaker from sitting around for so long, but he would rather push through discomfort than sit still with his thoughts all day. The isolation and silence were a punishment worse than death.

Once he was up and mobile, he began by gathering items around the cave and collecting supplies. His time as a farmer made labor a breeze, and his knowledge of survival was quite high despite living under a roof his entire life. He found the gathering peaceful and spent most of the day doing so.

He had collected enough materials to start making more permanent additions to the cave. He used stones to create a fire pit, providing them with a more sustainable place to cook and warm themselves at night. He also crafted a framed one on either side of the pit to hold a stick with food hanging off it, which allowed them to roast things more easily.

He carved tools out of stone and wood to make gathering more efficient and easier. He made fishing rods for them to use in the nearby creek and constructed traps to catch small game, providing them with a source of food beyond just berries and fruits picked from the trees. He even started working on crafting a bow for them to use, but the materials he had weren't the best.

After they collected a good supply of wood and supplies, Junius started to find ways to make living in the cave more comfortable. They had been sleeping on mats of leaves, which was better than the stone floor, but still not very comfortable. So, he used a series of vines to craft hammocks and secured them to cracks in the cave walls to support their weight.

By the time they were done, the cave looked much more homely than before. They had hammocks to sleep in, areas for storage to place wood, stone, and tools, and even a rack where they stored dried food.

Junius and Ehrindil had grown closer over the months they spent together. They began to feel more open about discussing their personal lives and started to trust one another beyond a superficial level. They even began teaching each other things.

Ehrindil was the first to bridge this gap. They were sitting in the cave, relaxing in their hammocks one night after enjoying a nice rabbit stew. They were both winding down but still wide awake, so they were killing time with small talk.

"We have made this arrangement quite cozy," Ehrindil noted aloud as he looked around at their cave. "I didn't expect this to be how I would spend my time hiding in the forest."

"It is nice," Junius agreed.

"Speaking of nice, that rabbit stew you made was fantastic. I didn't expect you to be such a culinary artist," Ehrindil praised.

Junius chuckled before saying, "I can't take credit for it. The recipe was my wife's. She was the master in the kitchen, I just tagged along and picked up the tricks of the trade."

Ehrindil looked over to see his expression shift from a smile to a blank stare. He interrupted the silence by saying, "You still haven't told me their names."

"Oh, right. My wife's name was Evonna. Our daughter was Aria," Junius answered.

"Those are beautiful names," Ehrindil complimented.

"That was also my wife's doing. She chose the name, and it was fitting. They were the most beautiful people in the world. Seeing their faces when I came in from the fields melted away my pain and problems. Everything was right in the world when I was with them," Junius explained.

"It sounds like you really have a wonderful family," Ehrindil stated.

"Had," Junius disagreed.

"You still have them, and you'll be reunited with them one day," Ehrindil said.

"I hope you're right," Junius sighed. "So, how did you get into magic anyway?"

"It's simple, I just started practicing," Ehrindil responded. "With the right patience, anyone can learn."

"What? What do you mean? I thought you had to be born with magic to use it," Junius said, confused.

"That's one way," Ehrindil elaborated. "See, there are three ways one can become a master of the magical arts. Through birthright, through research, or through service. Some people are born with incredible potential, some people must learn to harness the magic around us through tireless research, and others simply borrow their power from sources of incredible strength."

"Why not just borrow the power instead of spending so much time learning about it?" Junius asked.

"Because borrowing the power usually comes at an incredible price," Ehrindil replied ominously.

"Well, I can't lose any more, so show me where to get it," Junius added sarcastically.

"If you want, I can show you how to do a simple spell," Ehrindil offered.

"How?" Junius asked. "I haven't studied magic at all."

"It won't be anything harmful, but I can show you how to make a light out of thin air," Ehrindil said as he twirled his fingers, and a glowing orb of light appeared in his palm.

"I can give it a shot," Junius agreed.

"What you want to do is close your eyes and wave your hand back and forth. What do you feel?" Ehrindil asked.

"Air," Junius answered blankly.

"Precisely," Ehrindil exclaimed. "Air is what you've conditioned yourself to feel, but the air you're feeling is part of a greater web of life that flows all around us. It weaves its web between every crack of our existence," Ehrindil explained.

"I don't understand how that helps me," Junius said as he sat with his eyes closed, waving his hand back and forth.

"I want you to envision yourself waving your hand through a stream of magic instead of simply air. This is why I had you close your eyes, it helps you see what isn't visible," Ehrindil instructed. "Now, really think about the way the magic flows around your fingers and wraps around your arm as it slides through the fog of energy."

"Okay, now what?" Junius asked.

"Now I want you to catch the magic in your hand. It's no longer just air in front of you; it's raw power waiting to be harnessed. Grab it, and hold it in your hand. As soon as you do, command it to glow," Ehrindil guided.

Junius waved his hand back and forth and did his best to follow Ehrindil's instructions to the letter. He envisioned his hand flowing through a sea of prismatic particles and started to collect them in his palm. As soon as he did, he tried to turn it to light as he opened his eyes. Instead of creating a light in his hand like Ehrindil did, a bright flash of light pulsed and fizzled out almost immediately, to Junius' disappointment.

"Huzzah!" Ehrindil exclaimed, "Would you look at that!"

"What? All I did was make a flash. Hardly close to what you did," Junius said with a sigh.

"Yes, but you just skipped years of study and training. Some people have tried to do what you just did and couldn't without incredible studying. You pulled it off on your first try. I don't know if you're a natural or if I'm just a superb instructor," Ehrindil boasted. "I'm leaning more toward the latter."

Junius chuckled a bit before resting himself back in his hammock, saying, "Well, it was worth a shot. Maybe I'll shoot a fireball tomorrow."

"Don't get too hasty," Ehrindil warned. "Magic is immersively beautiful but can also be corrupting. Start with the basics."

"I was being sarcastic anyway," Junius dismissed. "Magic is outside of my area of expertise. I'm better with tools. Maybe I'll show you how to shoot a bow when I get this one done."

"I would rather enjoy that," Ehrindil said with a smile.

"We should probably rest, it's getting late," Junius suggested.

"No, I agree. I've droned on about the arcane for long enough," Ehrindil sighed.

The two of them nestled into place and rested their minds for the night. Ehrindil was impressed with how Junius was able to grasp the concept of wizardry so easily, even without prior practice or study. And despite how small the flash of light was, Junius was surprised he was able to do anything at all.

They drifted off to sleep to the sounds of the creek running in the distance, but the peaceful sleep was short-lived. After a few hours, Junius began to toss and turn, his dreams riddled with nightmares and the screams of his family. He jolted awake in a panicked sweat and looked around to see he was still in the cave.

It took some time for him to calm down, but eventually he caught his breath and his heart rate lowered. He knew better than to try to go back to sleep. He didn't want to see any more of the faces that waited for him once he closed his eyes, so he decided to get busy instead. He grabbed the pieces he had been molding for the bow and took them outside the cave to avoid disturbing Ehrindil.

As the sun rose, Ehrindil exited the cave to find Junius sitting on the ground and whittling away at some sticks. There were ten sticks laid out around him, all carved to a fine point at the end. The back of the sticks had feathers fixed to them with twine. Junius turned to look at him, his eyes tired, and nodded in greeting.

"Nightmares again?" Ehrindil asked.

"Yeah," Junius answered.

"I'm sorry, friend," Ehrindil said.

"On the positive side, I finished the bow," Junius pointed out. "I found some tracks not too far from here yesterday. Want to go hunt a boar?"

"That sounds barbaric... I'm in," Ehrindil replied.

Junius cracked a grin as he grabbed his bow and the arrows he was able to put together. He led Ehrindil farther east, all the way to the river where they would fish, and stopped at the spot where he last saw the tracks. He knelt and began searching for anything that stood out, focusing on the wetter part of the soil first to see if anything had been recently through.

"What precisely are you looking for?' Ehrindil asked.

"Anything, really. Footprints, flattened grass, or even piles of feces," Junius answered.

"Disgusting," Ehrindil responded.

"Maybe, but it can provide clues as to what we're hunting. But, this works fine too," Junius said as he pointed to a fresh set of tracks.

"Ooh, footprints!" Ehrindil exclaimed.

"They look fresh, let's stay quiet until we catch up," Junius instructed.

They both went silent and started to follow the tracks, doing their best not to startle their prize at the end of the trail. It took some time and patience, but eventually they found a few wild boars in a clearing ahead of them.

Junius held his fingers to his lips to signal him to stay perfectly still as he lined up his shot. He nocked the arrow, drew the bow, and aimed. He took a deep breath and let it out slowly as he was about to release the arrow, but then a twig snapped behind him. He saw the boar look over at them, so he fired as quickly as he could. The arrow missed its mark, and the boar started sprinting away.

"Damn," Junius muttered. "What happened?"

Junius turned to look at Ehrindil to find out why he had moved instead of listening, but was startled to see Ehrindil standing with a knife to his throat. There was a man behind him who was ready to slice him open. Ehrindil looked terrified.

"Drop the bow, and the knife, and anything else ya have on ya," the man said from behind Ehrindil.

"O-okay," Junius agreed as he started putting everything on the ground. "Take what you want, just please don't do anything drastic.

The memories of being robbed on the road started to rush through his mind, and the terrifying panic of what may come after flooded his emotions. His heart began to race, and his breathing grew rapid.

"Step away from the goods," the man ordered. "If ya try anything, ya friend here is as good as dead."

"No need for anything like that, I'll do what you say," Junius pleaded, not wanting to see another person killed.

"May I ask why you're doing this?" Ehrindil questioned.

"No," the man snarled, "Keep talking and I'll kill ya. If ya stupid enough to come hunting on my turf, then ya deserve whatever happens."

"I'll give you everything I have, please just let us go," Junius begged.

"I'll do what I want with ya," the man threatened.

Junius looked at Ehrindil, who suddenly seemed surprisingly calm. Ehrindil looked back at him and winked. Junius had no clue what he planned, but knew it was a bad idea. His eyes grew wide with fear as he saw Ehrindil start to twirl his fingers.

Suddenly, there was an astounding flash of disorienting light. Ehrindil copied Junius' flash and used it to blind the man temporarily. Then he pushed his arm away from him to twist and break free from his grasp. Junius reacted on impulse and ran in to grab the man's wrist, trying to isolate and steal the knife.

The man crashed his opposite hand into Junius' head, but he didn't let go. He then hit Junius again, but this time felt the sting of flames strike him in the cheek. The man turned to see Ehrindil preparing to attack again, so he crushed a third punch into Junius' face, knocking him to the ground.

Ehrindil blasted another bolt of flames toward the man, striking him in the wrist and knocking the knife from his hand. The man shook his hand in pain, but darted toward Ehrindil and grabbed him by the throat. He lifted Ehrindil off the ground with both hands and started to choke the life out of him. Ehrindil gargled and tried to breathe, but the pressure was too great. He kicked, punched, and scratched at the man, but he wasn't letting go.

Ehrindil could feel the light fading from his vision and the strength draining from his limbs. His eyes started to roll into the back of his head when suddenly he felt the man let go, and he gasped for breath. He coughed violently after he slammed into the ground, and struggled to get his bearings back. His limbs were shaky, and his vision was blurry, but after a few moments, he began to regain his senses. After he did, he looked over and saw Junius standing over the man with bloody hands.

Junius looked down at what he had done. There were multiple stab wounds in the man's back, and he wasn't breathing. He looked at his hands in disbelief; they were covered in someone else's blood. He had taken someone's life for the first time.

"Are you okay?" Ehrindil asked as he stood to his feet.

"I can't believe what just happened. What have I done?" Junius replied.

"You did what you had to," Ehrindil stated.

"Why did you do that?" Junius asked.

"You had worked quite diligently on that bow. I would hate to see some ruffian get his hands on it before you could put it to use," Ehrindil said as he winced.

Junius heard the pain in his voice and looked up at him, quickly realizing something was wrong. Blood soaked the lower portion of Ehrindil's robe, and there was a clear knife hole through the robe just over the lower part of his abdomen. Junius quickly jumped to his feet and rushed over to him.

"What happened?" Junius asked.

"It would seem he was quicker than I anticipated," Ehrindil said with a chuckle before he fell to one knee. "That is quite a painful wound."

Ehrindil placed his hand over the injury and began to use his magic to seal it, but focusing while in pain was difficult, and his expression bore witness to that. After the wound was closed, Ehrindil started to cough violently yet again, and fell to his hands.

"Ehrindil, stop moving. Let me carry you," Junius insisted.

"I would hate to be a burden," Ehrindil denied.

"This isn't the time for jokes, Ehrindil," Junius said as he reached down and grabbed his friend by the arms.

Junius muscled Ehrindil over his shoulders and started to carry him. He could feel the warmth of his blood beginning to soak into his own clothes, but he didn't care. All he could think about was getting Ehrindil back to the cave to rest. He didn't want to lose another person, even if it was a man he had just met a few months prior.

He quickly paced, one foot after the other, back toward their home. He didn't even think about grabbing his supplies, so all of that was lying on the ground next to the first life Junius had ever taken. His mind was a whirlwind of emotion, but saving Ehrindil was at the forefront of his thoughts.

Chapter 8

The trip back to the cave was significantly longer than the trip out. With Ehrindil on his back, traversing across the rough terrain was difficult, and his legs burned as he carried the weight of two people. But he pressed on, because there were no alternatives.

Throughout the trip, Junius did his best to keep Ehrindil talking, but halfway back, he fell silent. Junius could still hear him breathing, so he knew he was alive, but he worried about the extent of the blood loss. He also wondered how deep the cut was on his stomach.

Just before nightfall, Junius stepped through the cave entrance and stumbled over to Ehrindil's hammock. He laid him down and grabbed some water from the bucket. He soaked a rag and ripped away Ehrindil's robe to reveal the wound. The cut was mostly healed, but not entirely. In his weakened state, Ehrindil lacked the focus to complete the process.

Junius began to tend to the wound, cleaning it and preparing a holistic remedy to apply over the cut. He crushed some of the herbs and leaves they collected and combined them with a bit of water to make a paste. He then placed the paste over the wound to seal it and prevent infection, while also assisting the body's natural healing process. This process took nearly an hour, but he didn't stop until it was done.

After he tended to the wound, Junius had done all that he could do. He stepped back and wiped the sweat from his brow before looking at his new friend with worry. He let out a slow breath to try to calm himself before he turned to climb into his hammock. However, as soon as he raised a leg to climb in, his other one collapsed underneath him, and he fell to the floor. He didn't have the strength left to climb, and after he fell, he didn't have the strength to stand back up.

He rolled over to his back and looked up at his hammock. His body was tired, and he was ready for sleep, but he worried about his friend. He reassured himself that he had done all that he could and was sure it would work. Ehrindil would be awake in the morning. After that, he closed his eyes and drifted off to sleep.

The next morning came quickly. After such an exhausting walk back, Junius' body needed plenty of rest to recover, so it was already hours into daylight before he finally awoke. When he did, he sat up quickly and looked over at Ehrindil. He saw that his friend was still breathing, but still sleeping, which was better than being dead.

Junius' legs were sore, but his strength had come back to him with some rest. He walked over to their drying rack to grab a piece of dried meat. He took it outside and started to eat as he looked around for some more supplies to begin making another bow. The process was tedious, but he had no better option. He was afraid to go back to the one he left in case the man he killed had friends who might be looking for him.

As he finished his food, he took a closer look at himself and saw how covered in blood he was. His hands had been cleaned from the rags he used the night before, but his arms and body were still drenched in blood. A shiver traveled up and down his spine as he walked toward the creek to rinse off.

He dwelled on what happened for a long time. He didn't know what came over him, or why he reacted so violently. It was like his body was moving without his input as he ran toward the man and grabbed the knife. He remembered plunging the blade into the back of the man's neck, which was enough to kill him. However, he continued to stab him over and over, almost like he wanted to inflict as much harm as possible. The thought of killing coming so naturally was scary, because he didn't want to feel like he was anything like the men who ruined his life.

He made his way into the creek fully clothed and lay down in the water. They were in a dryer season, so the water was only a few inches deep at its shallowest points, and he just wanted to feel the flow wrap around him. He stayed in that position, looking at the canopy of trees above him for some time before finally moving to deeper waters to rinse off. Once he was finished, he took off his clothes and carried them back to the cave to dry.

He hung his clothes on a drying rack and placed it next to the fire pit before he started the fire. Without Ehrindil, he had to start the fire without magic, but he had everything he needed. He didn't let the convenience of Ehrindil's magic stop him from gathering the materials he needed to survive.

After he started the fire, he went over to check on Ehrindil. He was still breathing, but his pulse wasn't as strong as he would have hoped. It would seem the loss of blood was more severe than he thought. He removed the dressing he had made and checked on the wound. He was pleased to see that the paste he had concocted was working well, and the wound seemed to be healing nicely.

"Hang in there, Ehrindil," Junius muttered as he placed the dressing back over the wound.

The day was quiet, and Junius was slightly on edge most of the time. Any strange noises or movements he caught out of the corner of his eye would spike his anxiety. He worried that they were followed back, and that he would be ill-prepared to fight anyone off. The only thing that eased his mind was how much time had passed. If they truly were followed, they would have killed them the first night while they slept.

Junius carried on with his usual daily tasks, collecting supplies, preparing food, and cleaning up around the cave. As the sun was starting to set, Junius put his clothes back on and settled into his hammock. He wasn't tired just yet, but there was nothing better for him to do, and another good night's rest would hopefully be all Ehrindil needed to wake up. He closed his eyes and listened to the creek flowing as he drifted off to sleep.

Suddenly, his eyes shot open as he heard something moving outside the cave. He sat up immediately and looked into the entrance of the cave, where he saw someone standing with the moonlight at their back. The person was small, much too small to be an adult human, but he stared cautiously nonetheless.

"Daddy?" the figure spoke out.

"Aria?" Junius asked in a panic as he scrambled from his hammock. "Aria, is that you?!"

"Yes, daddy. Where have you been?" Aria asked.

Junius ran toward her and fell to the ground on his knees as he grabbed his daughter and pulled her close. He squeezed her tightly as he began to sob into her shoulder.

"I've missed you so much," Junius said through tears. "Where is mommy?"

"She's with the shadow people," Aria responded.

Junius' eyes immediately widened with worry. He placed his hands on Aria's shoulders and slowly leaned back from her, letting the moonlight illuminate her face. His stomach sank in horror as he saw blackened eyes and charred skin.

"We both are daddy," Aria said. Her voice suddenly shifted to a demonically terrifying tone as she shouted, "And you will be too!"

Junius gasped for air as he sat up in his hammock. He looked at the entrance to the cave as his breathing slowly returned to normal. He wiped the sweat from his forehead as he stared out into the nothingness.

"Having a bad dream?" Ehrindil said from the hammock.

"Oh, you're finally awake, I was beginn-," Junius stopped mid-sentence as he turned toward Ehrindil.

He looked at the hammock Ehrindil was in and saw he wasn't there. Instead, there was a different man. The man was shadowy in appearance, but looked as though he had elven features. He was sharply dressed and appeared to be lounging in the spot where Ehrindil once sat.

"Who are you? Where is Ehrindil?" Junius asked.

"Ehrindil is back home, where he belongs," the man said.

"What? What do you mean? Is he okay?" Junius asked.

"Relax, Junius," the man said as he sat up and looked across the room. "He is perfectly fine. My name is Dargothur, and I'm a good friend of Ehrindil's."

"A good friend?" Junius thought to himself, "Is this the one he said would come looking for him one day? It doesn't look like someone I would imagine Ehrindil being associated with. But how else would he know my name?"

"You did a good job patching him up, thank you for that," Dargothur said, interrupting Junius' train of thought.

"It was the least I could do," Junius replied. "How do I know you're telling the truth? Can I talk to him?"

"He's already gone home, I'm afraid talking to him isn't an option, but I can assure you he is healthy. He told me to pass along his thanks to you for all that you've done. He said he will find a pristine bow from his world to send to you," Dargothur explained.

Junius realized the man couldn't be lying, but it still didn't explain why he would leave without saying goodbye. He wanted to see Ehrindil as proof, but he had no right to make demands. They had only known each other for a few months after all.

"This is just another dream, you're not really here," Junius said, shaking his head. He had fallen for enough of his own mind's tricks for the day.

Dargothur interrupted, saying, "Oh, I can assure you that I am as real as they come. Tell me, Junius. What do you most desire?"

"That's a strange thing to ask," Junius replied. "Why?"

"I have quite a vast array of powers. There isn't much I can't do. Considering Ehrindil found you in this cave nearly dead, I would assume there is some unfinished business?"

"Can you bring people back from the dead?" Junius asked.

"Sadly, no, that power is reserved for those at the peak of existence," Dargothur answered.

"Then there is nothing I need, just leave me here," Junius dismissed.

"What will you do next?" Dargothur asked.

"I don't know. I'll figure it out," Junius answered.

"You don't plan to stay in this cave the rest of your life, do you? Or do you still plan on killing yourself?" Dargothur prodded.

"I don't know," Junius answered. "What does it matter to you? Are you worried I'll disgrace those I've lost as well?"

"No, no, no. I'm nothing like Ehrindil," Dargothur said slyly. "I think an eye for an eye is the best method of justice."

"What do you mean?" Junius asked.

"I mean, instead of killing yourself, why don't you kill those who took everything from you?" Dargothur asked.

"If only it were that easy," Junius huffed.

"But it is. You see, I can lend you my power. Then you will have the ability to exact your revenge," Dargothur offered.

Junius remembered Ehrindil's warning. He recalled that the price of borrowing power was usually incredibly steep. He looked out of the corner of his eye at Dargothur and could tell he was serious. Something about him felt powerful; it was almost frightening.

"How?" Junius asked.

"Simple, we strike a deal," Dargothur answered.

"What kind of deal?" Junius asked.

"The kind where you become the strongest person on the planet," Dargothur answered. "I will lend you the full extent of my power for you to use as you wish, the only things I ask for in return are the souls you reap from this world. Oh, as well as yours."

"Mine?" Junius asked, startled.

"Yes," Dargothur replied coldly.

"That's too much to ask," Junius replied.

"Think about it, Junius," Dargothur said as he walked toward him. "You could ram a sword through the hearts of all those who wronged you. You could inflict the same pain on those who harmed your family."

"Don't talk about them," Junius snapped. "I don't know why Ehrindil would have told you so much, but I don't know you, and you don't know them."

"Very well," Dargothur ceded. "I am merely trying to present you with the opportunity for change."

"Well, I'm not interested," Junius dismissed. "Go back with Ehrindil and leave me here."

"What will you do now?" Dargothur asked.

"I'll figure it out," Junius said as he stared at the floor in front of him.

"Well, if you change your mind, simply call out to me. You will find my ear can hear quite a distance," Dargothur offered.

"Don't hold your breath," Junius stated.

Dargothur snapped his fingers, and a red light appeared at his feet for a brief moment before flashing brightly and fading back into nothing, taking Dargothur with it. Junius was shocked at what he saw, but knew magic users had abilities he could never fathom.

He sat and stared at the ground for a while. With Ehrindil gone, he wasn't sure what to do. His sole purpose for living had been to help Ehrindil hide and survive until his friend came to get him. Now that that was done, what was left? He considered his options, debated on going through with ending his own life, but Ehrindil's words stuck with him. He let his head fall backward as he looked up at the ceiling.

"Evonna, if you can hear me, I'm so sorry I wasn't there. If I could trade places with you, I would. If I could take back everything I did, I would. I want to be where you are, but I'm not sure if you'll want me there. Can you forgive me for what I've done? Would you forgive me if I took my own life? Or can you not rest until your murderers are dealt with?" Junius asked aloud, hoping someone would answer, but there was nothing but silence. "I wish I could talk to you one more time. I've always been bad at decisions, but you always knew what we needed to do. I know you would have the answers…"

He let out a sigh as he let his head rock forward, and he looked back out of the cave's mouth. He could see that sunrise wasn't too far away, and knew he wouldn't be able to sleep anymore. He looked over at their food rack and saw they had no more dried meat, so he decided he would get an early start on gathering.

He grabbed some supplies, including a rod for fishing, and started out of the cave. He knew if he started early enough, he would be able to set some traps and catch some rabbits before lunch. He considered a nice rabbit stew in his future.

As he walked around the area where they prowled for food, he started to set up traps. He rigged a few of them up and then found himself at the riverbank, where he carried Junius across. He stared at it for a while and considered crossing to grab his bow, but the idea of someone waiting for him was unshakeable, so he never did. Instead, he tossed his line into the river and started fishing.

He sat there for a couple of hours with no real luck. Aside from a few nibbles and tiny fish, he saw no activity on his line. That suddenly changed just as he was about to call it a day. He grabbed his rod and started to pull in the line, but the hook wouldn't budge. He thought he was hung on a rock or maybe a sunken log, but then it started to pull away from him.

He scrambled to grab the rod to try and give himself more leverage on pulling whatever it was in, but it wasn't moving easily. He fought to get every inch he could, slowly winding the vine around the two wooden dowels he fashioned to the end of the rod, pinching his finger more than once in the process.

It took almost an hour of fighting, but eventually the fish began to tire, and Junius was able to pull in the largest fish he had ever caught in his life. He relished in joy at the act alone, which only doubled once he considered how big of a meal was in his future. He lugged the fish out of the water to get a better look at it.

The fish was as long as he was tall, and probably weighed close to his weight as well. It was a rare fish, and its meat was considered a delicacy, so he was excited to get to try it for the first time. He pulled out a stone knife and stabbed the fish in the head to save it from suffering a slow death by suffocation.

It took some effort, but Junius carried the heavy fish back to camp. He plopped it down on the stone just outside and began to filet the fish. Despite the creature's large size, there were only two real areas where untainted edible meat could be taken, the rest is typically mixed with toxins that blend with the tissue when the fish is under stress. However, cutting the good meat was an easy task with patience, and it would still be a huge meal.

Once he carved out two large chunks of meat, he set them over a fire and began to cook the food. His mouth watered at the sight. For the first time in a long time, he actually looked forward to something. He grabbed the fish's carcass and dragged it far away, so the smell wouldn't attract any predators, and so it wouldn't stink up his cave. He pulled it for about twenty minutes until he hit a deeper part of the creek nearby and tossed the fish inside.

"There, something else will have a nice meal too," Junius thought to himself.

He cleaned off his knife and hands in the water before starting back toward his cave. He was excited to get his hands on a fish that only the luckiest of Altomirians have had the opportunity of having before. He wondered if he should make a stew with it or just have the fish alone, but his wonderment turned to worry as he walked closer to his cave.

Shadows flickered outside of the cave, cast by the fire that warmed the walls, but the shadows were of a person. At first, Junius wondered if Dargothur had come back, but he didn't want to walk in unprepared. He grabbed the stone knife from his waist and slowly crept around the corner until he could peek his head inside.

What he saw both scared and infuriated him. There was a scrawny man inside, wearing dirty shorts, with his ribs showing. The man was clearly starving, but was armed with a blood-covered knife. The man was kneeling by the fire, tearing into one of the chunks of fish, utterly unaware of Junius' presence.

Junius took a moment to assess the situation and then started to calm himself. The man needed food, and there was far too much for him to eat alone anyway, so it wasn't a big deal. Besides, there was still another filet of meat hanging over the fire that was ready to eat.

"Hey," Junius announced from the entrance.

The man snapped his attention behind him and quickly jumped to his feet as he grabbed his knife, shouting, "Get away from here, this is my find!"

"And this is my cave," Junius stated. "Look, I caught that fish myself and brought it all the way back here to eat. But there is too much for me to eat alone, so you're welcome to the rest of the half you have. I have no interest in fighting."

The man looked down at the fish in his hand, then at the other half of the fish hanging above the flames before saying, "No, I think I'll take both."

"What?" Junius snapped. "What do you mean you'll take both?"

"I mean, I'll take both, are you thick in the skull?" the man responded.

"You couldn't possibly eat all that," Junius argued.

"So?" the man laughed. "I want it anyway."

"Why?" Junius asked.

"Because it's mine," the man snarled. "In fact, this cave is mine now, too. Yeah, all this stuff is mine."

"No, I've spent months building this, you can't have it," Junius argued, feeling a heat well up inside of him.

"Well, I'm taking it anyway," the man laughed. "It's human nature out here, survival of the fittest. If you're not strong enough, you'll always be beaten by people who are. And look at you, I can see you shaking from here."

Junius looked at the man standing around everything he had worked to build. The man was right, though; his legs were shaking. He didn't want to fight, but he didn't want to let everything he worked for slip away. He had already lost everything once; the idea of losing it all again was infuriating.

He tried to calm himself, but he could feel anger welling up inside of him. He hated the life he lived. He hated the evil people on his planet. He hated the fact that evil men took advantage of everyone, and no one ever did anything about it. But most of all, he hated that he was too weak to do anything about it.

"Leave here," the man shouted. "While I'm still feeling generous."

"No," Junius shouted back. "I won't let you."

"You don't have a choice," the man said, dropping the slab of fish and getting a firm grip on his knife.

"This is my cave, that is my bed, and that is my fish," Junius shouted as tears welled up in his eyes. "Get out of here NOW!"

"Are you going to cry?" the man said, taunting him. "You're so scared that even when you try to be brave, your body rejects it. What a coward."

Junius' heart beat rapidly, and his breathing was quick and shallow. He stared at the man through watery eyes. Maybe he was right, maybe he was a coward. Maybe he wasn't meant for conflict. Maybe he was destined to be robbed, beaten, and left with nothing.

"No," Junius thought to himself. "To hells with this. I'm not running anymore."

Junius started to approach the man quickly, his stride increasing with every step until he was nearly sprinting at him. The man was stunned, but readied himself to attack before Junius came within range. The man tried to swipe his knife at Junius' neck, but was surprised as Junius dropped his knife, ducked under the swing, and tackled him into the fire.

The heat from the charred logs was enough to burn his flesh. He screamed out in pain as he desperately tried to wrestle Junius off of him. He was eventually successful, but he didn't get back up on his feet. Junius threw a wild punch that landed flush on his jaw and dropped him to the ground in a flash.

Junius pushed the man over after he punched him, and fell to the ground with him. His movements were uncoordinated, as his body was tired from the labor of the day, but he was fueled by adrenaline and anger. The man in front of him felt like the representation of everything he hated in this world, and he wanted nothing more than to stop him.

As he fell with him, their heads collided, cutting open Junius' eye from the impact. But he ignored the cut and quickly scrambled to get on top of him. The thief was groggy from the multiple blows to the head. Between getting punched and bouncing his head off the ground, he was looking through a fog.

The man tried to stab his knife up at Junius, but his wrist was grabbed. The two of them struggled for a moment, locked in a stalemate, until the knife slowly started to twist toward the thief. When compared to the scrawny man, Junius was slightly larger and more nourished, so he was able to overpower him and win the fight for the blade. The thief tried his best to fight him off, but Junius was able to turn the knife downward and began to shove the blade into his throat.

The man pushed back as long as he could, but it only prolonged his death. The blade pressed against his skin, slowly building pressure until it cut him open and began to sink into his tissue. The knife severed vessels and organs before it finally started to press against his spine. By the time it did, the man's fate was already sealed, but Junius was unrelenting.

As the man's grip faded and the blade shoved entirely to the ground, Junius snatched the knife from his body and began to slam the weapon into the man's corpse repeatedly.

"Why didn't you just leave?!" Junius shouted between stabs. "You could have left me alone! I just wanted to be alone! We could have shared the damn FISH!"

Junius slammed the knife into the man's forehead and felt the blade bend as it struck the ground beneath his skull. He tried to pull it back, but it wouldn't budge. The tip had curved behind his head, making it too hard to pull free.

Junius fell backward from atop the dead man and looked at what he had done. His hands were covered in blood again, and he could feel blood falling from his face. His lip began to quiver as tears fell from his eyes once again. But this time, he wasn't distraught; he was angry. He was furious that the man made him kill him.

As the tears fell from his chin, he yelled out in frustration and sadness. Was this what his life had come down to? Killing everyone who threatened him until he couldn't, then dying himself. No, he wouldn't live like this; it wasn't worth it. So he made a choice then and there.

"DARGOTHUR!" Junius shouted at the top of his lungs. "DARGOTHUUUUR!"

He waited for a moment, but he didn't have to wait long. Just as the man said, a red flash of light appeared and brought him back to the cave in the blink of an eye. Dargothur stepped forward, but seemed unaffected by the dead man lying across from Junius.

"You called?" Dargothur asked.

"I don't want to live like this," Junius muttered as he stared at his blood-soaked hands. "I don't want to fight for my life every other month."

"You don't have to," Dargothur promised as he walked closer to Junius. "You can accept my offer and do something about it. Just imagine, you can take the fight to them. You can stop them before they get a chance to do these things again. You can not only save others, you can get revenge."

Junius began to absorb his words. The idea of hurting those who had hurt his family was more than just desirable; he craved it. The offer started to cut through his conscience like a hot knife through butter. The more Dargothur spoke, the more appealing it seemed. But was it worth his soul? What was the value of a soul anyway? Would giving up his soul be that bad? He struggled with the idea before, but after what just happened, the answers were clear.

Dargothur placed his hands on Junius' shoulder and leaned in close as he said, "You could cut down the bastards who burned your wife and daughter... Get revenge for Evonna and Aria, Junius. Take the deal and kill them, you've already broken through the barrier of what it's like to take another life, so what's the hesitation? Your family deserves justice."

Junius' eyes widened as he listened. He only paused for a moment before saying, "I accept."

A fiendish grin stretched across Dargothur's face from ear to ear as he said, "Excellent, Junius."

"How much power?" Junius asked.

"Excuse me?" Dargothur questioned.

Junius snapped around and looked Dargothur directly in the eyes, repeating, "How much power can you give me?"

"How much would you desire?" Dargothur asked.

"All of it," Junius responded.

"Let's not get ahead of ourselves. If I were to give you the full extent of my power right away, you would burn to a crisp from the inside out. The power I give you is measurable by the deeds you perform for me," Dargothur explained.

"What deeds?" Junius asked.

"It's quite simple, really. The more souls you collect for me, the stronger I will make you," Dargothur answered.

"How can I begin to get justice for my family if you won't give me enough power to do it?" Junius asked.

"You will start with more than enough of my power to exact your revenge on whoever you deem fit to deserve it," Dargothur declared as he stuck his hand out to shake Junius'.

Junius hesitated for a moment. He didn't know what was going to happen, but he knew as soon as he touched Dargothur's hand, the deal would be set in stone. He thought it over one last time before accepting that it was the only way he could get justice for his family. He placed his hand against Dargothur's and felt a surge of energy wash over his body.

The feeling was painful as it felt like flames were rushing through his veins, but it dissipated just as quickly as it started. As the pain subsided, Junius felt a strange feeling at the tips of his fingers. He looked down at his hands, trying to find the source of the tingling.

"That feeling you have, that's your power trying to escape," Dargothur explained.

"How do I use it?" Junius asked.

"Focus on that feeling in your fingers and follow it to your core," Dargothur instructed. "Once you do, you will bind with your ability, and its intricacies will be revealed to you."

Junius did what Dargothur said and followed the feeling up his arm and into the center of his body. He could feel a pestilent mass swirling around inside of him. As soon as he found it, the understanding of his power came flooding into his mind.

"What is this?" Junius asked.

"That is your mark. It will stay with you until you die, and then your soul will be transported to me. While you live, this is the source of your power. Feed it and it will grow, expanding your abilities and making you the strongest person on Altomir," Dargothur claimed. "I look forward to seeing how you use it."

"So now what?" Junius asked, expecting there to be more to this transaction.

"Now, well, now it is up to you. You have everything you need to finish the plan you've already conjured. You can live the fantasy of you standing over the corpses of those responsible for your family's death. The only thing between you and your goal is distance," Dargothur responded.

"What will you do?" Junius asked.

"Me? Oh, I have much more to tend to than this," Dargothur stated.

"Are you going back to join Ehrindil?" Junius asked.

"Yes, that's where I will be going next," Dargothur answered.

"Will I see you again before I die?" Junius asked.

"It all depends on how the dice fall," Dargothur said with a devilish smirk.

"Okay. If I can get back at those who hurt my family, I will be indebted to you," Junius stated.

"My dear Junius, you already are," Dargothur said as a flash of red light erupted beneath his feet and he disappeared.

Junius looked surprised as he watched the man vanish into thin air. He looked down at where Dargothur was standing and saw an etching in the stone floor, riddled with strange symbols and infernal designs. It was unlike anything he had ever seen before.

Junius looked at his hand again and then looked at the fire pit he had built. He held his palm out and focused the power within himself. Suddenly, he felt a surge of energy rise from the depths of his abdomen and grow in power as it collected in the palm of his hand. In a blast of green light, a powerful beam rocketed out of his hand and slammed into the firepit, blasting it to pieces.

Junius looked at the destruction, then back at his hand as a smirk stretched across his face. For the first time in his life, he had the abilities that could potentially match the most powerful people on Altomir. He wasn't drunk with power; he simply thirsted for vengeance.

He looked back at the hammock Ehrindil was in before mumbling, "I hope you're okay, and thank you for all that you did for me. I will find a way to pay you back someday."

Junius stood from his hammock to grab his things and some food. Even though the night still had hours left, he was ready to begin his trip back toward his home region of Altomir. He didn't fear anything in the woods and was unbothered by the thought of being attacked. He had a new list of abilities that he was itching to try, and anything or anyone unlucky enough to cross his path would be on the receiving end of his curiosity.

Chapter 9

Junius marched back through the forest with a newfound purpose and determination. Gone were the days of lying around waiting to die; instead, he would bring pain to those who so willingly harm others. He would be the great equalizer that Altomir needed, and he would quench his thirst for revenge at the same time.

As he walked, he thought deeply about what he was planning to do. He knew he had already damned his soul, and he knew his plans were far from being considered the right thing to do. However, he also knew that being the hero was unrealistic. The odds of living by a just set of moral principles and still being able to change the world's landscape were isolated peaks. Truly good people could only influence those around them and hope they follow in their footsteps. That was the only way good people could make change. No, he was going to do things more effectively. You could be good, or you could be an immediate change, and he had no intention of waiting around for the morals of Altomirians to correct themselves.

Throughout the next two days, he practiced harnessing his new powers by blasting attacks at trees and attempting to use more precise powers to catch small game for food. What he discovered was both fantastic and frightening to him. The abilities felt natural, as if he had been practicing them his entire life, but there was a clear limit to his strength.

Despite this, not everything he tried worked. He repeatedly attempted to harness the same portal magic that he saw Dargothur do, but it wouldn't work. He could feel the power starting, but it would always fizzle out before it manifested at his feet.

"One day," Junius thought to himself.

This practice consumed his every waking minute. He pushed the boundaries of what he could do, just to see what he could get away with. He couldn't harness all the elements like he would read about in stories, but his ability to blast caustic and powerful attacks was surprisingly potent. Some of his strikes would latch onto the bark of trees and begin eating away at them after impact.

By the time he found himself close to the edge of the forest, he had already been walking for a day and a half, and he stepped out onto a familiar stretch of road. He could tell he was between Coniston and his home, so he knew the bandits that haunted him were somewhere close by. They had been stalking that stretch of road for some time, so he decided to start looking.

He turned toward Coniston and began to march down the center of the road, looking for any signs of the bandits. He walked for an hour before he saw anything or anyone else on the road. However, it wasn't the bandits he walked up toward; it was where he was beaten nearly to death.

He saw Ippy's remains where they were when he was killed. Scavengers had picked apart his corpse, so he wasn't recognizable. Flies had taken over what little was left of the body at this point, and the smell was repulsive. The pieces of his wagon had been taken as well, leaving nothing behind but the bones of the dead horse.

Rage festered inside of him, only fueling his desire to find the men responsible, and he marched onward. He told himself he would pace the road between his home and

Coniston a thousand times if he needed to, knowing he would eventually run into them.

After many more hours of walking, he could see some smoke rising from chimneys in the distance. The sun was beginning to set, so he told himself he would rest in Coniston for the night. The village was no more than another hour away, and his feet were starting to get sore. Despite his determination, he was still human, and his body continued to suffer from fatigue.

As he started to try to relax his mind, a voice rang from the shadows that spiked his heart rate and sent his nerves on edge. He could recognize the voice from anywhere, and his jaw clenched tight enough to hurt his teeth. He turned his attention toward the sound of the voice and saw four men step from the shadows.

"Well, well, well. Look what we have here, boys," a man announced to his allies.

"Isn't that the rat we robbed and beat to death?" one of the other men asked.

"Clearly not enough, he's still alive and healthy," a third man spoke.

"Tell me, rat, do you feel like you've learned somethin'?" the man asked as they walked closer to Junius. "Do you feel like a lesson was taught?"

Junius didn't respond. He searched desperately for this exact moment, but as soon as he saw the four men, he felt something he didn't expect. He felt fear.

"You see, we were kind to you. Despite you lashin' out with needless violence, we didn't kill you. We simply took what was ours and made our way up the road," the man said threateningly. "In all reality, we should have killed you."

The four men closed the distance and were only a few feet away as their leader stood mere inches away from Junius. The bandit stared him directly in the eyes, but Junius kept his gaze low and aimed at his feet.

"What's the matter? Can't look me in the eyes? Are you so riddled with guilt for what you made us do to your horse that you can't bear to look at me?" the leader taunted. "Do you still wanna hit me?"

Junius didn't respond. He was experiencing a whirlwind of emotion and was frozen in place. He wanted to lash out, but the repercussions of his actions last time began to crush down on him like a boulder of guilt. He wasn't expecting to feel so much anxiety and terror.

"It's impolite to ignore your superiors," the bandit growled before he punched Junius in the stomach.

The attack was strong enough to knock the wind out of Junius and force him to buckle to his knees. He began to cough as he tried to catch his breath, and the other three bandits all laughed at the sight.

"I think we'll take whatever you have in your pockets. You seem frail, and we want to lighten your load again," the bandit laughed as he started to search Junius' pockets. At first, he didn't find anything, but eventually, he grazed his fingers across the drawing Aria had made and yanked it from his pocket.

"No!" Junius shouted, but he still hadn't caught his breath.

The bandit kicked him in the face to knock him over and started to unfold the paper. He looked at the drawing for a moment before he burst out in laughter. He held it up for the other bandits to see, and they all joined in.

"You mean to tell me that was your home we found? Damn, you have some bad luck," the bandit said with torturous glee. "To think, we lightened you of so many of your burdens. You really should be thankin' us. Now you don't have to work your fields, feed a kid, or keep a bitch wife happy."

In that moment, something snapped in Junius, and his pain vanished. The fear he felt evaporated, and it seemed as though his body was acting on its own. He reacted in a blur, and the only thing he could hear was the calm but thunderous beating of his heart in his ears. He held his palm out and blasted a ferocious beam of energy at the bandit leader's knee, blowing through his limb and separating his lower leg from his body. The bandit yelled out in agony from the attack, and the others were stunned.

Junius jumped to his feet and began to lash out silently. He didn't make a sound; he simply locked onto his targets with his only intention being to kill. The bandits all drew their weapons as quickly as they could, but they stood no chance.

Junius looked at the first bandit and locked eyes with him. He reached out and pulled toward him as if he were yanking the air away, and the bandit began to panic.

"I can't see, what the hell?!? Why did it get so dark?" the bandit shouted as he tried desperately to feel around.

The other two looked at the blind bandit and then back at Junius, who locked eyes with another one. Junius pointed at the ground, and the bandit he stared at suddenly started to kneel.

"What's going on?" the bandit shouted. "I can't control my body!"

"Demon," the final bandit whispered.

The last bandit dropped his sword and turned to run away. He sprinted as fast as he could toward the treeline, desperately trying to escape Junius' line of sight. He was only a few feet away from the forest when he felt a sharp pain on the back of his head and a loud popping sound in his ears that rang loudly and disoriented him. Suddenly, his legs gave out from underneath him, and he fell to the ground. That's when he saw pieces of his brain fall onto the grass in front of him. Within seconds, he was dead.

Junius looked at the blinded bandit and threw his hand forward again, unleashing the fury of the hells as four rapid blasts of fire flew from his fingertips and slammed into the bandit, one after the other. The bandit was quickly engulfed in flames and ran around mindlessly, trying to put it out. The screaming was harrowing, but Junius didn't flinch.

The kneeling bandit desperately tried to stand up, but his body wouldn't listen. It was like his limbs were under Junius' control and bowed to his command. He watched as Junius walked menacingly toward him, the screams of his friends ringing in his ears, and he began to panic.

"Please, please don't kill me. I'll do anything you want, please!" the bandit pleaded.

Junius reached down and grabbed the sword that had been dropped on the ground and looked at it, deciding what to do next. He ignored the kneeling bandit's pleas for mercy and placed the tip of the sword on his throat. He slowly began to push the blade into the man's neck at a glacial pace, forcing him to endure as much pain as possible, before he finally stopped breathing and fell to the ground.

The leader rolled around on the ground, yelling in pain as he tried to stop the bleeding from his leg. He heard the screams of his friends slowly fade into silence as he tightly tied a rag around his thigh to stop his blood loss. That's when he heard Junius' footsteps grow louder as he drew closer. He looked up and saw Junius reaching down to grab the drawing, and helplessness began to take over his soul.

"Who are you?" the bandit asked.

"I am a product of your immorality. You made me. I am the reaper of the damned souls that don't deserve to live in the filthy husks they call a body. I will cleanse Altomir of your filth as if you were nothing more than dirt on the floor of my home," Junius muttered in response. "I am here to kill you."

"Please, let me live and I'll tell you anything you want to know," the bandit begged.

"You no longer have the numbers or the overwhelming power, and now you want to beg for mercy?" Junius asked as he held his palm out toward the bandit. "Tell me, how many people have begged you for that same mercy, and you didn't give it to them? How many people have you slaughtered in cold blood? You don't deserve mercy, you deserve death."

"Wait, please, wait!" the bandit shouted. "I know who's responsible for your farm!"

Junius hesitated for a moment and lowered his arm, growling, "Speak, dog."

"I'll tell you if you promise to let me live," the bandits bargained.

"Fine, talk," Junius demanded.

"It was Bokon. He told us to burn the farmlands to the east, and not to let anyone leave. He figured if the farmlands were burned, but not the farmers, they would just make more. He ordered us to kill," the bandit explained.

"Bokon, your leader?" Junius asked.

"Yes," he answered.

"Where is he?" Junius asked.

"H-he's… in Sanctuary," the man hesitantly responded.

"How many people are with him?" Junius asked.

"Hundreds, maybe more," the bandit answered.

"Good," Junius responded as he raised his hand again.

"Wait! You said if I talked, you would let me live," the bandit pleaded desperately.

"I lied," Junius replied coldly.

Junius released another stream of hellfire that engulfed the bandit and coated his skin. The flames burned as hot as the magma that flowed from the Vulcus Mountains to the west,

116

and Junius stared at the bandit until his screams stopped from underneath the inferno.

"May your souls rot in the bog of hell," Junius snarled as he stared at the melting corpse.

He decided against going into Coniston. Instead, he stepped off the path and started moving westward. He knew where Sanctuary was, even if he had never been before. He knew it was a heavily fortified city with giant walls and strong defenses. He had heard that whoever held Sanctuary held the seat of power in the region. But he didn't care. There could have been a million bandits hiding within the walls, and he would still walk in to raze it to the ground.

The longer he traveled, the more determined he grew to end the Clan of Phantoms. He wouldn't just cut off the head of the snake; he would destroy the entire organization. No one left to replace Bokon meant there would be no more Phantoms. He thought about it and was determined to kill them, but still wasn't sure how he would do it. His powers were great, but not enough to contest hundreds of people at once, especially if some of them were powerful magic users.

That's when an idea struck him. His power would grow the more lives he took, and the closer he got to Sanctuary, the more bandits he would see. The more bandits he killed, the more people he inadvertently saved, so it was a winning solution in his mind. So, he decided to kill every single roaming bandit group he came across.

It took a couple of days before he saw the first group. Before then, his waking hours were spent gathering food and water for his journey. He knew it would take around a week to get there, so he had to be prepared. However, on his second day of travel, he spotted his first group of bandits.

Only three men were walking in a small group, but they were armed and wearing traditional attire that the Clan of Phantoms wore. He wasted no time in dispatching them as quickly as possible, burning them in a sea of hellfire and collecting their souls. The men never even saw Junius coming.

Junius continued this pattern, more and more, the closer he drew to his target. Not everyone he killed belonged to the Clan of Phantoms. There were a couple of squads from the Brotherhood of Anarchy, as well as one from God's Judgement. But Junius didn't discriminate. A bandit's life was meaningless, useful for nothing more than growing his power and broadening his capabilities to take down even more. The guilt he once felt for taking a life was gone, and his body count began to skyrocket.

Throughout his journey, Junius never interrogated anyone. He ignored their pleas for help, but he did try to end them swiftly. He wanted the bandits who killed his family to suffer, but the rest were simply stains that needed cleaning. They were worth nothing more than the effort required to kill them.

By the time Junius could see Sanctuary on the horizon, he had killed over a hundred men. He could feel power flowing through him in ways it wasn't before, and he knew his plan was working. The more lives he took, the more unstoppable he felt, and the more eager he was to flatten the walled city.

On the night of his eighth day of travel, he found himself standing just up the hill from Sanctuary. The city sat atop steep cliffs that dropped for hundreds of feet on three of its sides, with the back side of the city positioned right next to a mountain. The large walls of the city towered in the distance across a wide ravine that separated him from the main gate.

There was a bridge that connected Sanctuary to the other side, but a small outpost guarded the end of the bridge. Sanctuary truly was as fortified as possible.

Junius looked out at the city and smirked. It was time to put his strength to the test.

Chapter 10

Junius' hands began to tremble as streaks of red magic started to spark from the tips of his fingers. He had collected an incredible number of souls, and he only had one power he wanted to use. He held his hand out, and Sanctuary began to flash, creating an awe-inspiring display of crimson light. The flashes numbered in the hundreds, and illuminated the streets as if it were daylight, until finally they stopped.

Within seconds of the flashing beginning, the screaming of battle started. Junius smiled as his plan worked, and he could hear the slaughtering of everyone inside. Each flash of light was a portal to another realm. He didn't care what he brought over, as long as something came intending to do damage. He used the portal magic he saw Dargothur using, but in reverse. Instead of transporting him somewhere, he brought danger to his location.

The screams and dim torchlight began to shift as hordes of monstrosities and demonic creatures began to rip everyone to shreds. Fires started to engulf homes, looking as though someone had lit bonfires behind the walls. Junius waited for a few minutes before he began to approach the outpost. He wanted the Clan of Phantoms to bite on the distraction before he came. And when he started to feel the surge of souls flowing from within the walls, he knew it was time.

Junius walked up to the gate and blasted it open, creating a straight path for him to follow to get to the bridge. A titanic creature was inside the outpost, ripping everyone to shreds. A dozen dead monsters were lying around, but multiple dozen bandits joined the pile of corpses. Junius ignored the battle, stepped over the dead, and crossed the bridge.

As he approached the front gate of Sanctuary, he started to slam his attacks into the door to break it open. There were three guards posted on the wall above him, but he didn't care. Before they could turn their bows on him, a ferocious howl of otherworldly proportions echoed from farther down the wall. The echo was followed by the screams of the guards as they were ripped to pieces. One of their mangled corpses slammed into the ground next to Junius as he broke open the front gate.

Junius entered the city and began walking up the cobblestone streets, which were coated in blood. The intense battle between man and monster raged around him, but he ignored it entirely. He set his attention on the building farthest back, as he knew Bokon would be hiding in there. He stepped over the bodies of bandits and walked through streams of blackened blood as he continued his path unbothered.

He was surprised at how resilient the bandits were to his attack. He assumed their reaction would be slow, considering the invasion was abrupt and unlike anything they could have prepared for. But, there were plenty of dead monsters in the growing mound of corpses that littered Sanctuary, giving credence to the strength the Clan of Phantoms possessed.

However, Junius didn't care. Their numbers were finite, and no matter how many monsters it took, he could keep summoning them. Sooner or later, every soul in Sanctuary would be claimed for his use. Once they were dead, he would leave the city as a haunting warning for anyone who dared to follow.

Eventually, Junius found himself outside the front door of the building he assumed Bokon was in. He saw two guards standing outside the building. One had a pike in his hand, and the other held two small flames, one in each palm.

"Get back to your house, we're under siege by monsters!" the man with the pike shouted.

Junius didn't respond. He targeted the magic user and slammed a precise bolt into his forehead, blowing the back of his head off and ending any potential magical threat.

The pike-wielding guard looked at the other in horror as he shouted, "What the h-"

Junius killed him in the same fashion, clearing his path to the door. He walked up the set of steps and tried to push the door open, but it was locked. He stepped to the side and blasted the handle. As the door swung open, it was immediately engulfed by a monstrous stream of flames that burned the wood to a crisp. The sound of metal clanking on the ground rang out as the hardware fell from the charred timber.

Junius looked closely at the metal on the railing and could see the faint glow of a fire in someone's palm. He looked at the reflection closely before he jumped into the doorway and blasted another pinpoint beam of magic directly into the mouth of the man who attacked with the flames. Once he had passed the ambush, he looked deeper into the room and saw that only one man remained on the opposite side.

As the man's body fell to the ground, the other spoke from across the large room, "Are you the one responsible for all this commotion?"

"Are you Bokon?" Junius asked.

"I am," he responded. "Who are you with? Burgrunde? Magnus? Or that snake, Jadeshot? No, it couldn't be Jadeshot, he doesn't possess the guts to try this. So, Magnus?"

"I don't belong to any bandit group, nor do I work for any filth like you," Junius shouted.

"Then you're a fresh face in the sea of those who've tried to take this place," Bokon said as he stood to his feet, almost unamused. "You will die just like the rest."

"I don't care about your pathetic posturing. I'm here to kill you for what you've done to me," Junius yelled angrily. "You took everything from me. My friends, my horse, my goods, my home, and my family! You will pay for every moment I don't get to spend with them, and then your soul will burn in hell."

Bokon laughed and said, "You seem to hate me dearly, but you're not alone. You're no different than the thousands of others who feel the same. And just like all of them, you're nameless, a nobody. Let that be a testament to how foolish your goals of conquest are. I am infamous for changing lives, and no one knows who you even are."

"Before you draw your final breath, you will," Junius snapped as he blasted an attack straight for Bokon's head.

The attack rocketed through the air at a blistering speed, rattling the room as it shot through the wall with enough force to leave only a small hole. But Bokon was untouched; he seemed to have vanished into thin air before the attack landed.

Junius looked around frantically for him, but didn't see him anywhere. He started to spin in circles, desperately searching for any sign of his enemy, but all he found was empty space, and all he could hear was Bokon's disembodied laughter echoing off each wall of the room.

"You look frightened, poor boy," Bokon spoke from seemingly every direction. "It appears you didn't do your research. You thought you could walk in here blindly and take me down? Did you foolishly assume it was the walls of Sanctuary that kept everyone from taking my throne? There's a reason I'm called the King of Phantoms."

Suddenly, Junius felt a stinging sensation across his lower back. He winced in pain and quickly turned around, but no one was there. Just a small tuft of pale green smoke that quickly diluted into the air around it. Junius placed his hand over the sting and felt he was cut open.

"So, let me guess," Bokon's voice rang out again. "You ran a shop that my men stole from, and someone fought back?"

Junius felt another slice across his left arm and heard his fabric tear as he was cut, but aside from another pale green tuft of smoke, there was nothing. It was as if he had been cut from nowhere and by nothing, yet he suffered an injury all the same.

"No, you don't look like a shopkeeper. You look like you work a life of labor. Your pathetic yet sturdy frame is a testament to that. Maybe you were a miller and my men decided to relieve you of your supplies," Bokon guessed again.

For the third time, Junius felt another slice, this time across his cheek. He could tell that Bokon was toying with him. Any of those attacks could have been at his throat, but instead they were in non-vital areas as if Bokon was trying to instill fear before going for the kill.

The plan was starting to work. As Junius realized the deep water he was in, panic began to rise in his chest. Despite his recent comfort with killing, he was still inexperienced in battle. A leader of a bandit faction would be the opposite, and now he could tell.

"Oh, I think I know now. You must be a farmer," Bokon said ominously as Junius' eyes widened. "I'm willing to guess you're from the east, past the river. I bet you have some farmland out there, and my boys came and burned it, you, and your family down.

"Shut your damn mouth!" Junius shouted as he started to rapidly fire flames in every direction, dousing the walls in hellfire that stuck to them like burning tar.

Bokon laughed loudly before slicing Junius across the stomach. Junius saw the tuft of smoke milliseconds before he was cut, but he wasn't fast enough to try to counter. By the time he processed what was going on, he was already bleeding.

"That's it, isn't it? Tell me, did they scream when they died?" Bokon taunted, relishing in Junius' misery. "Did they squeal as their bodies were fried to a crisp? Did they stay awake long enough for the flames to melt their flesh? Or did the smoke get to them first?"

"Come out and show yourself, you coward!" Junius shouted as he continued to launch attacks in multiple directions.

Streams of scorching flames followed blasts of powerful green magic. Within a minute, the walls of the room were completely covered in flames. The fire was beginning to stretch up to the ceiling, but their fight raged on.

No matter how many attacks Junius threw, Bokon avoided them all. However, Junius was suffering blow after blow, slicing his body open all over. Blood fell from his fingertips and pooled in his boots from the dozens of wounds he had suffered. He was beginning to grow desperate and worried he might die.

In his desperation, Junius started to call upon his summoning powers. He created two portals in the room, hoping something with a keen sense of detection would appear. What he saw was frightening.

A demonic-looking humanoid appeared alongside a hunched-over canine-shaped creature. Both of them were dark colored, had leathery skin, and demonic red eyes. Their flesh looked hardened like stone, and their teeth were jagged in appearance. The demonic-looking creatures appeared and immediately started searching around the room they were in.

Junius observed the demons, hoping to use their perception to find Bokon and land an attack of his own. The canine-looking demon snapped its attention to its left, but a moment too late. The human-like demon suddenly grabbed its neck as black blood poured out over its fingers. It fell to the ground and bled out quickly.

For the first time in the entire fight, Junius saw Bokon attack. The tuft of smoke was nothing more than a diversionary tactic meant to distract exceptionally keen enemies. Bokon actually attacks from the opposite side and cuts with a strange blade that appears to be the same smoky, pale green color as his distraction.

However, knowing how he attacks still doesn't help him combat the speed at which he does it. Even if he were to catch the smoke, he could never react fast enough to land a strike before Bokon disappeared again.

Junius looked at the last demon closely. It was hunched over and scanning around when it suddenly snapped its attention toward him. Junius reacted as quickly as possible and ducked while stepping backward. The dodge worked perfectly, and for a brief moment, Bokon and he locked eyes before the bandit vanished yet again.

"That's not very sportsmanlike of you," Bokon spoke aloud. "This was supposed to be a test of fates between two men, yet you bring these puppets here to help you?"

A yelp rang out around the room as Bokon said the word 'puppets'. The canine demon fell to the ground with a massive gash across the nape of its neck, and it wasn't moving. Bokon had easily dispatched his demon allies.

"You really should save as much dignity as possible. I would hate for you to die a fool and a coward," Bokon continued. "But enough of this banter, you've already made a mess of my city. It's time to end this."

Junius was breathing heavily and running out of options. He knew he could be cut open at any moment, so he started to react irrationally. He began to duck and stumble all over the room, hoping to dodge whatever attacks Bokon might throw. His strategy was odd, but it did seem to buy him some time.

"I see you've decided to die a coward after all, you're not as powerful as I thought you'd be," Bokon growled.

As he fumbled around sloppily, Bokon attacked him more than once. His erratic running and ducking did save him from getting his neck sliced open, but it didn't save him from harm. As Junius ran around, he was cut across the back and stabbed in the side. Both of these strikes were significantly more harmful than before, but neither was enough to kill him.

Finally, Junius was starting to run out of stamina, and the blood loss was beginning to take its toll. He left a trail of blood all over the room, and his clothes were saturated. If he didn't receive medical attention soon, he would succumb to his injuries. He collapsed at the foot of Bokon's throne and turned to look out at the rest of the room.

Bokon reappeared in the middle of the room and started to walk toward him. He had a sword in one hand and a dagger in the other. Both of them looked like smoke contained in a glass case, but they cut like razor blades. He held them out to his side as he relished in his victory and slowly paced toward Junius.

"Do you smell the iron in the air? The musk of blood and fear is like an aphrodisiac to me. There is truly nothing like it. Desperation may as well be an appetizer, while the look in your eyes as you draw your last breath will be the main course," Bokon threatened as he walked up to Junius. He knelt beside him and whispered quietly to him, "Let me tell you something, the savory flavor of a man so desperate to kill you but too weak to do it is unlike any other. I've enjoyed this."

Junius smirked, which vexed Bokon and made him hesitate for a brief moment. He looked down and saw Junius had his palm flat on the ground, and then saw a bright ring of red light appear around his palm.

"You should run," Junius muttered as he lifted his hand.

Suddenly, the ground erupted in a pillar of fire that nearly reached the ceiling. Bokon jumped backward to avoid the attack and was about to laugh at Junius' feeble attempt when he felt another one blast upward from beneath him. He dashed to the side, but yet another pillar of flame consumed where he was standing.

No matter where he stepped, it seemed he found himself in yet another attack. He moved at an incredible pace, but nearly every step was met with an identical inferno. He watched Junius as he quickly fled, and was stunned to see that he had stood and was taking aim.

Junius started to blast his powerful beams at Bokon. Each attack smashed into the wall behind him and blew through the stone, creating a hole large enough to crawl through. Bokon was doing well to avoid these attacks as he tried to figure out how the flames were coming from underground when he saw a faint green light coming from beneath him.

That's when he felt something he had never felt before. The pillar wasn't a stream of flames like it had been before. Instead, one of Junius' beam attacks erupted from the ground, which moved significantly faster than the fire. He had grown used to the timing of the flames, so he wasn't moving fast enough to avoid the beam, and his leg paid the price.

The beam ripped into Bokon's calf, tearing at his muscle and breaking his bone. Bokon fell to the ground and growled in pain, but didn't slow his pace. As he slid across the ground, he hurled his dagger at Junius, but the attack was dodged. Junius retaliated by blasting Bokon in the elbow with another beam, ripping apart his arm at the socket.

Bokon howled in agony, but reached out with his right hand. Junius aimed another attack but was abruptly interrupted as the dagger Bokon threw slammed into his back, piercing his lung. He tried to breathe, but every breath felt like it was cutting at his insides. Junius reached behind him and grabbed the handle of the dagger to pull out the blade. He tossed it to the side and started to cough up blood.

Junius saw Bokon reaching his hand out again, and the dagger began to slide across the ground, so he shot another beam of magic at Bokon's right elbow, blowing his arm apart at the socket yet again. Bokon screamed in pain as he looked down at his body. Both of his arms and one of his legs were gone, and he was losing blood even faster than Junius was. He let out a defeated sigh, as he knew he had been beaten.

Junius limped over to him and knelt. He looked at the state Bokon was in and smirked before he spit in Bokon's face, saying, "All that posturing and look at you now. You underestimated me."

"It would seem I did," Bokon mumbled, looking Junius in the eyes.

The inferno raged around them as the walls had become fully consumed by the fire. The holes Junius blasted into the stone acted as vents to fan the flames and increase their intensity. Despite its sturdy structure, the building would likely collapse before long, burying whoever was inside.

"You weren't that hard to figure out, and you were too arrogant to think I even could. First, I noticed your attack patterns when you went after the demons. That's also when I realized you take whatever is near you into your phantom state with you. A piece of my robe appeared next to the dog after you tried to attack me. That would mean going into your phantom state while surrounded by flames would be too dangerous to you.

So I decided to rig this entire floor with traps. I'm willing to bet you thought I was running for my life, but I was placing dozens of traps for you to stumble through. None of which were set to arm until I triggered them. In the midst of these were a few special traps. I figured you would have the timing of the flame traps fairly quickly, but you would be too distracted to make the necessary adjustments. It was only a matter of time before I took one of your legs," Junius explained.

"What the hell are you explaining all of this for?" Bokon snarled.

Junius leaned in close to him with a sinister look in his eyes and said, "Because... the savory taste of a man so desperate to kill me but too weak to do it is unlike any other. You were right about that much at least."

Junius stood to his feet and blasted all of Bokon's wounds with searing flames that cauterized his vessels and stopped him from bleeding. Bokon bit down and endured the pain, trying not to give Junius the satisfaction of his torment. After the attack was over, Junius started to walk toward the door.

"Where are you going?" Bokon barked.

"Enjoy your final moments, Bokon," Junius said over his shoulder as he walked to the door. "I wonder if you'll succumb to the smoke, or if you'll stay alive long enough for the flames to melt your skin. Your end is the same either way. You'll die here, a smoldering corpse."

"Get back here and finish what you started," Bokon demanded, yelling louder the farther away Junius walked. "Are you too scared to kill me yourself? Too weak? What's the matter? Don't you want vengeance for your family?!"

Junius walked through the doorway and out into the street. He knew Bokon had nowhere to go, and that the flames would be on top of him soon. He wanted him to suffer as much as possible before he drew his last breath. He did his best to ignore his own injuries, but he knew he would need medical attention as soon as possible. He wasn't sure where he would find it, but his adrenaline allowed him to act without care.

The screams and howls of bandits and monsters still echoed around Sanctuary, but there was significantly less of it than before. The blood flowed between the stones like a crimson river, and the bodies littered the alleyways. Homes were lit with flames that stretched into the sky, and some were already starting to crumble.

He continued to slowly walk toward the gate of the city, across the bridge, through the ruined outpost, and up the hill to where he started the raid. He turned back toward the city and looked at the destruction he had brought. The city burned brightly against the night sky as the flames began to consume everything inside. Monsters and men alike were overwhelmed by the flames as they jumped from building to building. Roofs began to collapse from the heat, eventually followed by the largest building toppling in on itself.

Junius took a breath to soak in his victory, knowing that Bokon was dead and that the Clan of Phantoms had been dealt an irreparable blow. The breath he took was painful, and he started to cough violently, spitting blood in the process.

"You should see a healer," Dargothur's voice rang out as he stepped from the shadows.

"I plan to," Junius answered, not breaking his gaze from the inferno.

"You pulled it off," Dargothur said as he looked at the flames. "I have to admit, I thought you would die here. Seems like your soul lives to fight another day. I also have to admit, your use of the portals is unorthodox, but effective."

"So it seems," Junius responded.

"Well, now that you have your vengeance, what will you do next?" Dargothur asked.

"I haven't gotten my vengeance," Junius replied.

Dargothur looked at him confused and asked, "Is that so? Who is left to kill?"

"Mathius," Junius answered coldly. "If he hadn't turned me away, Evonna and Aria would still be breathing. Tell me, how far can I travel with these portals?"

"With the amount of souls you've collected, I'd say you could go anywhere you want at this point," Dargothur answered.

"Good," Junius said. "I'm leaving Altomir for Paxanthus. After speaking with Bokon, I know the evil of this world runs too deep to cure alone. I could kill every bandit faction, and more would take their place. The common people are too weak to defend themselves against organized crime here. I will kill Mathius and carve a path for Altomirians to travel through who seek shelter. Mathius himself told me that he can only control travel to Paxanthus through that singular gateway, a foolish piece of information to tell a stranger, so I know I can get in undetected. I will use Paxanthus to create a haven for the good people here. And once I do, well, then I can die peacefully. You'll have my soul, and I'll have my peace."

"Mathius will not be so easy to kill, the Overseer is a bastion of peace and power on Paxanthus," Dargothur warned.

"I will spend the rest of my life preparing if I need to. Eventually, Mathius WILL die by my hand. My wife and daughter deserve justice for what they suffered, and he is the last one who must pay," Junius declared.

He pulled the drawing Aria made for him from his jacket once more. He stared at it, but this time his heart did not shatter. He ran his fingers along the page, wishing he could hold them again. A painful lump grew in his throat, but it was followed by anger. He wanted the heads of everyone he felt was responsible.

"I will bring Mathius to justice for both of you," Junius whispered. "If it takes my last breath, I will avenge the pain you suffered."

He folded the drawing and placed it back in his jacket. Then he held his hand down and took a breath, the portal marking etched into the soil beneath his feet, and a flash of red light consumed his body. In the blink of an eye, he vanished, leaving Dargothur standing there alone.

A wicked smile stretched across Dargothur's face, which grew into laughter. His laughter grew louder and louder before he finally said, "It looks like I will get the souls I want after all, Elijah. Let's see you stop me now."

Dargothur vanished alongside Junius, leaving nothing behind but the etchings on the ground. His sinister plan was unfolding better than he had hoped.

Sanctuary crumbled to ruin overnight, leaving nothing but the walls standing where the city once reigned supreme. Magnus Corvus and a large force of his bandits arrived to raid the city a few days later, and found nothing but ruins. He wasted no time in taking control of the city and began to rebuild Sanctuary in his own image, thereby granting himself the seat of power in the region.

The Brotherhood of Anarchy and the Midnight Eclipse also spread their influence, dividing the region into three nearly equal parts that they would fight over for years to come. All three of the bandit leaders were young and ambitious, and with Bokon gone, they all had an equal chance in the war to come.

All three of the remaining factions laid claim to eliminating Bokon and burning down Sanctuary. The only one of the three that could prove anything was Magnus, as he held his position at Sanctuary and took over in Bokon's stead. However, this didn't stop the others from claiming they were responsible, and no one dared to question it for fear of death.

Despite the end of the most dangerous faction around, the oppressive force of bandit presence never truly faded. After a couple of years of the other clans growing in strength, the criminal presence was greater than it had ever been. The common people of Altomir had little chance of ever living without the threat of violence if they stepped out of line.

However, Junius hoped to fix that problem sooner rather than later…

TO BE CONTINUED…

If you enjoyed the story, I would love to hear your thoughts! Reviews are the best way to help small authors like me spread the word about our stories!

Supplementary Information

Brotherhood of Anarchy

A vicious organization that is run by a woman named **Burgrunde**. The faction is merciless and short tempered. They strike down whoever they choose, whenever they want to, and only respect power. If you are too weak to stand up to them, you are too weak to live. They take whatever they want from the people inside their territory, and regularly send raiding parties to those on the outskirts of their domain.

Midnight Eclipse

A shadowy bandit clan run by a man named **Jadeshot** The weakest of the three warring bandit factions, but the worst one to cross. They prefer to operate in the shadows, and will let their enemies think they've won. As soon as they let their guard down, they will strike in the night and eliminate their threats. They will use poison, espionage, shadows, and any trickery they can to beat their foes, but they avoid open combat, opting instead to flee and regroup if they can.

God's Judgement

A heretical organization that is run by a man named **Magnus Corvus** The strongest of the three warring factions (after **Bokon** was killed). The people in God's Judgment feel they are on a divine mission to purge weakness and blasphemy from Altomir. Their members are the most unpredictable. Sometimes they are working alongside the people in their domain, toiling and helping them, and other times they are sacrificing village elders because they felt it was necessary. The people under them live in constant fear, and dare not to even speak out of line about their rulers lest they face the executioner's axe.

Clan of Phantoms

A grim and savage organization that once held the most powerful seat amongst the bandit factions. It was run by a man named **Bokon** and nearly wiped out the other three factions when it suddenly vanished. When their capitol building was investigated, they found it razed to the ground and everyone inside was killed. No one knows who wiped them out, but all three of the other bandit factions lay claim to the victory. Since the clan has been destroyed, the power vacuum has led to the other three factions clamoring for control.

Altomir:

A ravaged planet filled with bandit factions that are constantly battling over control of any and all territory. The people of Altomir rarely have any allegiance to these factions, but rebelling against them has proven to have worse outcomes than simply abiding by their rules. Any strong young men and women who could potentially stand up to them are either killed or they leave to join their ranks.

Magic is almost non-existent on Altomir, and any magic users typically climb the ranks of a bandit organization quickly. The three most powerful magic users on Altomir are all leaders of their respective organizations. There is no government and no policing force anywhere on Altomir, as any who have tried to form these organizations have been quickly killed off and their followers made to be slaves.